INDIAN TIME

A Novel
of Western Oklahoma

ALSO BY CHARLES R. PENOI

NO MORE BUFFALOES

INDIAN TIME
A Novel
of Western Oklahoma

CHARLES R. PENOI, Ed.D

Pueblo Publishing Press
Yukon, Oklahoma

ISBN 0-942316-07-X

Library of Congress Catalog Card Number: 84-60603

Second Edition, February, 1987

Cover Painting by Jerome Bushyhead

Pueblo Publishing Press
Yukon, Oklahoma

To My Anadarko Buddies

Bob Lawrence
Raymond Manschreck
Robert Swank

FOREWORD

Western Oklahoma is a hard country. Its rolling hills are dotted with scrub oak trees. The constant wind, either from the north or the south, drives some people to despair. For this reason, the men who have stayed on are a tough breed. The womenfolks are a shade more feminine, but not weak.

Native Americans were here first—they are still here. The whites and Native Americans tolerate each other, each with a deep distrust. Things are a little better now, but not much. Newspapers in this part of the world still play up the role of "Lo, the poor Indian." Actually those days are a long distance behind us.

I have drawn from the things I know best, Indian culture, especially the Plains Indian culture, along with non-Indian culture. And there is an element of both the old and the new; there is a shaman and a soldier from Viet Nam.

This story is fiction, the characters were created by me, so it could only be a happenstance if you see yourself here. Ku-ken-ish, a Laguna Pueblo Indian, was borrowed from the real world for this story. He was my grandfather.

There is a special vocabulary known only to Indians, the words are English, but the meaning is different. For example, "Osage exercise" means to take a nap after eating. "Indian time" means when you get there, or being late. In the story, when the time is given as, "When the rooster crows three times," the rooster doesn't have any signifigance, it just means, when you get there.

Writers often model their stories after their own lives. This is good and bad. Whatever, the story's the thing. It may be there is some beauty, some vulgarity, some lust, but so is life lived. We do not live in a perfect social atmosphere, we live as human beings, some part good, some evil. I always say, "The devil made me."

1

Jacob Hawkins had been schooled at Riverside Indian School, Oklahoma City University and the University of Chicago Divinity School. While going to school he met and married Ruth Price, a blond, blue-eyed Kansas girl. She had a similar background with one exception, she had been raised on a farm. She could milk a cow, pitch hay or run a tractor. She also leaned towards religion, that is what brought them together. One other thing, wherever she went she attracted stares. She was a beauty, not the run-of-the-mill beauty, but a knockout! She could have married her choice of men. She wanted Jacob!

Jacob had held small churches in Canton, Seiling and Clinton, Oklahoma. After two years of marriage a son was born. He too was named Jacob, but from the first he was called Jake.

Jake's education came from small town public schools through the eighth grade, then an Indian boarding school. He lived in two cultures. Like his father, Jake learned very fast.

Jake watched his father cope with various small town churches, but he felt that his father wasn't happy with his work. Often during the family meal he would catch his father wollgathering, but he didn't ask any questions.

Actually Jake felt closer to his mother in many ways. One summer evening when she started for her usual walk Jake said, "Mother, mind if I walk with you this evening?"

"No, I would enjoy it." In some ways she was lonesome. She missed the farm life, and the good-natured banter of her brother.

Jacob always appeared so serious.

Jake and his mother walked towards the creek. The soft, summer sounds and the rustle of the wind were soothing. After a few minutes Jake said, "Dad seems preoccupied, he doesn't seem happy with his work. What's wrong?"

Ruth Hawkins was slow in answering, and chose her words with care. "Your father is a well-educated man, and, like most men, he is ambitious. He feels like he is not being recognized for his efforts. It bothers him. I'm glad you wanted to walk with me. There have been times when I've felt like an outsider. I love your father very much, but because of his preoccupation with the church, we have become almost like strangers."

Jake had always taken it for granted that his mother and father were happy. They were his strength. "I'm sorry Mother, I haven't been much help to you. I'm not much good at giving affection, but I'll learn. You can teach me how."

This was pleasing and surprising to Ruth. Slowly and carefully she chose her words. "Love is a physical feeling. Everyone needs someone to care about them. I know your father loves me, he just doesn't show much affection."

I never thought about it too much. I thought both of you were very happy together."

"I'm happy in a way, so don't become upset. Your father and I have talked about going to Kansas where my family lives. He could probably get a church up there."

They stood by the bank of the creek awhile. After throwing in some rocks for effect, they started back. It was getting late. Night sounds always came across as new sounds. They heard whippoor-wills and a screech owl. As they neared the house Jake said, "Thanks, Mom. I enjoyed the talk and the walk."

Ruth smiled, "You haven't walked with me very often. We'll have to do it again."

Jake Hawkins and Robert Gombi were seniors at Riverside Indian School in Anadarko, Oklahoma. Jake was Kiowa on his father's side; Robert was Comanche.

Indian boarding schools are not country clubs. The hours in school and out are rigidly scheduled. Free time comes on the weekends. But Saturday morning was inspection time. If the matron thought they hadn't done a good job on their detail, she gave them hours, which meant a loss of free time. The boys knew that she was often hard to please, especially if someone had crossed her.

Her nickname was Big Eyes. The boys in their wing were almost men. When they showered, old Big Eyes often found it convenient to walk by the shower room door. For a while there was laughing and joking about the matron, but they became used to it and paid little attention to her.

The school year passed too quickly; suddenly it was spring. The superintendent knew that with graduation, hoards of parents and friends would descend on the school. He wanted it to look good.

Finally inspection was passed. After a hurried lunch they headed for the north hills. This was their refuge, their home away from home. They topped the highest ridge, dumped their canteens and food, and flopped on the ground. Lying on their backs they watched the fluffy clouds floating by. The soft spring breeze was just warm enough to make them sleepy. The sounds of insects, the rustling of leaves in the blackjacks was enough to put them to sleep. The distant sound of spring thunder was like the rhythm of truck tires. By now they were sleeping soundly.

Jake could hear voices in the background, he couldn't tell if they were real or not. It was like a movie; during one sequence he was at a school picnic, his classmates talking and joking, suddenly he was in the backseat of a car. The girl was beautiful, but everytime he moved toward her she vanished.

He and Robert were hitchhiking along Interstate I-40, but no one would stop. After what seemed like hours of walking, a Cadillac pulled over to the side of the road. A girl called, "Get in, boys."

Jake and Robert were so tired they stumbled into the car.

"I don't usually pick up hitchhikers, but I noticed you were Indian boys. What tribe are you?"

Finally Jake mumbled, "I'm Kiowa, my friend is Comanche."

The girl was driving with one hand, and turning to look at them in the back seat. My name is Mary Marie Tinker, I'm Osage. I inherited two head-rights, I'm eighteen, and on my own."

Jake could see that she was not a full blood. He could smell

3

the scent of perfume, with a trace of alcohol. Mary Marie kept driving with one hand, she kept turning around, talking in a loud voice. "Where are you boys from?"

Jake was assuming the role of spokesman, "I live near Anadarko, my friend lives around Lawton."

The faint sound of distant thunder aroused Jake, "What's the hurry, I have all afternoon." He turned over.

Again he and Robert were moving along in the Cadillac. The thing that worried him was Mary Marie's driving. Fortunately there were few cars on the road. Suddenly the car pulled over to the side of the road. It wasn't an easy stop. "You boys want a drink?"

"What do you have?"

"I have a bottle of Kentucky bourbon, the best money can buy." Jake and Robert looked at each other. Neither had tasted booze but they sure didn't want to appear like country boys.

"Well, as long as it is good stuff we will take a snort."

Mary Marie reached into her purse, brought out a bottle, and handed it to Jake. He took a big swallow, but choked and gagged. His throat felt like it was on fire. He handed it to Robert who did the same thing with the same results.

"How do you like my booze?"

Choking, sputtering, trying to breathe, they said, "We like it fine. Thanks so much."

"Want another drink?"

"No thanks, we are doing OK."

"It will put hair on your chest."

Both of the boys could suddenly feel the effect of the booze. They looked at each other and laughed. "Who ever heard of an Indian with hair on his chest?"

Mary Marie reached over the seat and patted Jake on the leg. "Don't you boys go to sleep on me."

"We won't." The world about was becoming more beautiful. Their eyes did not focus too well, but what they saw they liked.

Mary Marie took another drink from the bottle. "Have another drink, it will make you feel good."

Jake reached for the bottle and handed it to Robert who took a small swallow. Choking again, he handed it to Jake.

Mary Marie started the car and took off with a roar. The car was swaying back and forth. They were sober enough to know that one of them would have to drive or they would end up in a

4

ditch or have a wreck. "Stop the car!"

"What for? I'm the driver." She did slow the car down, then it came to a halt in a bar ditch.

Jake and Robert climbed out, they could see that the car was stuck. Shoving and pushing they made some progress, Mary Marie wasn't any help.

Robert looked over to a clump of trees, "Hey, I know this place, there is a lake over there. Let's go over and have a swim." All agreed this was a good idea.

This time Jake took over the wheel, with all three of them in the front seat. The small lake sparkled in the summer sun. Man, it would be good to go in. There was nothing like a good swim, with or without a swimsuit.

Jake pulled the car over to the bank of the lake and they all piled out. "Last one in is a dead dog."

As quick as lightning, all three literally ripped of their clothes. Robert, buck naked, ran for the lake.

"Help me, someone, my bra hooks are caught."

Jake stood there like a statue. He couldn't move.

"Don't just stand there, help me."

Fumbling, he got the hooks undone. In one move Mary Marie slid off her panties and ran for the lake. Jake couldn't move, his head was swimming. "Jesus, I never did see anything like that." Finally, he managed to get to the lake.

The blue sky had disappeared. There were streaks of lightning and a crash of thunder. Robert and Jake caught the full force of the rain. There was no use running as there was no cover. Jake muttered, "Jesus, what a dream! I would sure like to meet that Osage girl."

Spring was a good time and a bad time. The closing of the school year was good because now they could go home and make all of the powwows. It was a sad time because the seniors knew they would probably never see most of their classmates again.

The last days of school were a blaze of picnics, class parties, and group pictures. Boys and their girlfriends were sad. Both carried the fear that this was it.

One of the events that everyone looked forward to was the school powwow. This year Jake was to be the master of ceremonies, Robert was the head drummer. All of the girls had sent home for a shawl, a few even had buckskin dresses. Some of the boys wore costumes, but if they didn't have any it didn't matter. Jake introduced the Head Man Dancer, the Head Lady Dancer, the Head Little Girl Dancer, the Head Little Boy Dancer, the Head Singer, and Robert, the Head Drummer. This was one time the invitation didn't read BYOD&C (bring your own dishes and chairs) because everyone was invited to eat at the school cafeteria.

Jake started off with a gourd dance. In sequence he called for a straight dance, ladies' buckskin dress, ladies' cloth dress, wrapping it up with a round dance.

Student after student called, "Forty-nine!", but Jake didn't have the authority to extend the dance. The superintendent saved the day for him by announcing, "No forty-nine. The last dance will be the round dance." Students and guests surged forward, this was it.

School employees were posted around the dance to see that no one went to the bushes. Alert as they were, one or two couples did manage to find their love nest.

Graduation day was an anticlimax. It was hot, hot! Graduation gowns were warm, little beads of sweat rolled down the backs of the graduates. The school gym was like an oven, the speaker was loud, and full of hot air.

During the ceremony thunder clouds had developed in the west. A loud clap of thunder startled everyone. The superintendent hurridly lined up the graduates and called out their names. Heavyhearted, they trudged acorss the stage. School employees checked the seniors, relieving them of their caps and gowns. It was all too mechanical.

A government boarding school is unique. Many of the students spend their entire school years here, from grade one through grade twelve. It is like a giant family, students get to know each other in classes, dormitories and outside activities. Couples fall in love, out of love; occasionally a girl will be sent home because she is pregnant. Life goes on.

Seniors know it is all over, this is it. All of their emotional feelings show, especially sadness. Deep in their hearts they suddenly know they are alone. Choices have to be made: more schooling, pershaps marriage, work?

All of the feelings that had been submerged, surface. Girls who rarely cried, openly cried as if their hearts were coming apart.

Boys didn't know what to do, they formed circles and recalled the good times they'd had together.

School officials had chartered Greyhound busses to take many of the students home. Some parents had picked up their children early, this caused more confusion. School counselors worked frantically checking on each student's transportation.

Jake lived near Anadarko. You followed highway 9 west to Hog Creek and you were there. His parents had been at the graduation ceremony, but were going on to Oklahoma City for a church meeting. Now they were busy shaking hands, smiling, accepting congratulations. They were proud people.

Robert caught the Lawton bus. Although he did not have a girlfriend at school, the finality of graduation had hit him hard. He didn't want to talk, there wasn't anything to say. Glancing out the window of the bus, the panorama of spring was like a haunting memory. He and Jake had made their summer plans weeks before. They would go home for awhile where they would be honored by their parents; more shaking of hands, more good wishes. Then the real fun would start.

Jake had not said anything to Robert, but he intended to go to Osage county. That dream was too real—there must be a Mary Marie.

Getting from town to home was no problem for Jake, he had only to stand by the side of the road. This was Indian country. Indians almost always picked up other Indians. Walking west on Central Boulevard he took a left on Mission street. No sooner had he taken the turn than a car pulled up, "Want a ride?"

"Yeah."

The car was a 1970 four-door Impala Chevrolet, loaded with suitcases and boxes. He didn't see any place to sit. A small voice came over the boxes, "You sit here, Jake. I'll sit on your lap."

"OK."

The voice came from Darla Koumbi, a Commanche girl who was a classmate of his. Jake sank back in the seat, the cushions were about shot. With Darla on his lap the trip took on new meaning. She was a tall, long legged girl with hair as black as a raven, and a heart as black as sin. She kept wiggling and pressing against him. His arms were crowded for space, so it helped to hold Darla around the waist. With the crooked road and the bumps his arms would press against her breats; he could

7

feel his heart pumping and thumping. Darla didn't say anything, she just kept pressing and giggling. When they hit a big bump Jake got an armful.

"Oh, my God."

The driver turned around, giving Darla a quick look. "Are you hurt? I thought I heard you moan."

"Oh I'm alright." Secretly Darla enjoyed it. She kept pressing against Jake and giggling.

The driver slowed down. "Hog Creek church is around the bend, is that where you want off?"

"Yes, sir."

Soon the driver pulled over to let Jake out. Jake felt like a sandwich. Darla sighed, she hated to lose her passenger.

"I'm having a dance Saturday, will you come?"

"Yeah, I'll come. Where is it?"

"Comanche Junction, five miles east of Cache. You can stay with my family."

"OK. I'll be there."

As Jake walked to the house he was thinking, "Darla certainly isn't Mary Marie, but she will do."

Entering his room he sighed with pleasure at being home again. He undressed, except for his shorts, and piled on top of his bed. In a few minutes he was asleep.

After all the time at Riverside it was nice to be at home. The one thing he noticed most of all was the peaceful quiet, no clanging bells, no shouting students. He could sleep as long as he wished, it was like being in heaven.

Heaven soon wore off. He had explored, slept, and talked to his family. They went their way and he was left alone. By Saturday Jake was ready to head for Comanche Junction.

That evening at supper, when there was a lull in the conversation, Jake asked, "Dad, can I use the pickup Saturday?"

"What do you plan on doing?"

"One of my classmates wants me to come to her honoring powwow."

"Tell me about it."

"The girl's name is Darla Koumbi, she lives at Comanche Junction west of Cache."

"Do you know her family?"

"No, I only know her as a classmate at Riverside."

8

"What is she like?"

"I really don't know that much about her except what I have told you. Do you think I should go?"

"Jake, life is full of situations that come up. Decision making is not easy, but I am going to leave it up to you. You can use the pickup."

"One other thing, she wants me to spend the night with her folks."

Jacob looked at his wife, both were wondering if Jake could handle it. "The answer is still yours. If you think you can manage, it's alright with me."

That was all that was said. Jake helped his mother with the dishes, hoping she would say something. "What do you think, Mom?"

"It's like your father said. Physically you are almost grown, but your experience with girls hasn't been all that much."

"What do you mean?"

"All girls are not honest. Often they want to get married, and getting pregnant aids their goal."

"Isn't that taking a chance?"

"Yes it is. Girls these days don't seem to mind if they are married or not. Do you know about human reproduction?"

"We studied about reproduction in our course in biology."

"Did they teach you anything about contraceptives?"

"No." Jake felt a slight blush creeping over his face.

"Jake, sexuality is good when the couple is old enough to understand what it is all about. Too often young couples only want one thing, themselves, this often leads to trouble. We have some books on sexuality and marriage, it might be a good thing for you to read them. If you have any questions we will be glad to answer them."

"OK."

"Jake, the physical relationship between husband and wife can be very beautiful. It is when people are lacking knowledge about their bodies that they get into trouble. You have a good time and enjoy your trip. Anything else?"

"No. And thanks."

Jake was surprised at the ease with which his mother talked to him. His mother was beautiful in more ways than one. He felt lucky to have such parents.

Like the winds that swept down from the north, the winds of change in Jake's life were sending a mixture of joy, happiness, sadness. Nothing was the same. The expectations that he had looked forward to had disappeared. He didn't understand it, from all appearances it should be the greatest.

"To hell with it, I'm going. I'm sure there will be some of my friends at the powwow."

Jake spent Friday washing and cleaning the pickup. He checked the tires, oil and gas, the tank was almost full. That should get him there and back.

By Saturday morning Jake was packed, his old suitcase held the extra clothes he would need. It would be hot, dancing always made you sweat. At breakfast with his family his younger brother teased him about his girlfriend. "She is not my girlfriend, she is just a friend."

As he was leaving, his mother gave him a big hug. "Be careful, there are lots of accidents these days. There will probably be some drinking, so play it safe."

"I will, Mother."

Jake's father walked to the pickup with him. He reached for his billfold, pulled out a twenty dollare bill and handed it to Jake. "Have a good time, but remember, perfume and booze have got many a man in trouble."

"Thanks, I'll remember."

Pulling onto Highway 9 he headed south. The blacktop road reflected heatwaves. It was such a great day. He rolled the window down. Western music flowed from the radio. It was good to be alive.

Mile after mile passed. Sunflowers along the road swayed in the south breeze. Oklahoma blue skies were washed after the spring rain. Puffy, white clouds moved with the south wind. There was almost no one on the road. Small birds pecked at the grain that had fallen from grain trucks. Up ahead Jake could see grain elevators jutting into the sky. They were the skyscrapers of the plains.

Jake wished for a coke, it would wake him up a little. Soon a country store conveniently appeared. He pulled over and stopped. "Where is your coke box?"

"Yonder in the corner, help yourself. Put the money on the

counter, I have to pump some gas." Some rural towns still had pumps for filling gas tanks.

"It's been a long time since I've seen a pump like that."

"Young feller, this isn't one of those fancy stations where everything is run by electricity; if it goes off you are out of business. This old pump never goes out of business. It will be here and working as long as I'm around."

"How far is it to Cache?"

"Not far. Lawton is just down the road a piece. Keep to the right at the first turnoff, that will take you to Cache. It's about a thirty minute drive."

It was so peaceful resting on the old wooden bench. A few cars drifted by.

"Not much going on these days. Folks want to stop at fancy stations or use self-service."

"I guess it's a little cheaper that way."

"It's just a gimmick. Everyone these days has a gimmick, sometimes I think that's what life is all about."

"What's the matter, old-timer."

"Who's an old-timer? Crazy kids, men and women living around with anybody they can get in bed. When I was a young man we didn't have anything like that. When we wanted a woman we married her."

"Didn't the men ever sleep around?"

"No sir, there was none of that foolishness." Looking towards the range of hills, the old man stood still. Jake could see tears running down his face. "God damn it, how did I get started on such a subject?" Turning towards Jake the old man stared into his eyes. "My daughter took up with a soldier from the fort. Last time I heard of her she was someplace in Texas. Never married or nothin', just took off. I hope to hell both of them starve to death."

Jake found words difficult. "You wouldn't take your daughter back?"

"Well, maybe I would. It's easy to give advice and sound off, but I'm lonely. The wife is dead, and this was our only child. Towards evening I go up yonder and visit my wife where she's buried. I put wild flowers on her grave. You know, I'm glad you stopped. I sure have been soundin' off." He looked up at the hills again. "Yes, I guess I would take her back, it's so lonely. The years have caught up with me, and I sure would like to see her again."

11

"Well, old-timer, I've got to be moving along."

"If you are ever in this part of the country again, stop in. Next time the coke will be free."

"Thanks." Smiling, Jake shook hands with the old man.

"Take care, young man."

Pulling out on the highway again, Jake headed for Comanche Junction. Like the old man said, he took a right at the edge of Lawton. The only difference he noticed in this part of the country was that the soil was a different color, it was almost white. The soil around Cache was not good for crops, but it grew enough grass for the rancher's herds.

That day Cache baked in the sun. Not a creature stirred. One or two dogs lay in the street, when they heard a car coming they would get up until it passed, then they would return to their sleeping. Cache was only a block long. Jake headed west, and when he had counted five section lines, he looked for a mailbox that said, Koumbi. He noticed one mailbox tilting on its side. so he stopped and walked over to it. Sure enough, it said Koumbi. He noticed a wire gate with a tin sign hanging on it that read, Chew Mail Pouch for That Wonderful Feeling. There was a rutted road leading south, and in the distance a clump of trees and a stone house.

Jake pulled the wire hitch from around the gatepost, then pulled the gate back beyond the road. He drove the pickup through the gate, then wired it shut again. As he followed the road he saw the house begin to take shape. All of the houses in this part of the country were made out of rock, as rocks were in abundance. Timber was scarce, also it was expensive. The only cost for a rock house was the labor and some cross beams. There were plenty of rocks. With a little cement you could build what you wanted.

The farther south Jake went the larger the house became. "Man, Darla didn't tell me her old man was loaded, he must run alot of cattle." Jake drove up to the house and got out of the pickup. He had been riding so long that his knees seemed paralyzed. Walking up on the porch, he knocked on the door. He could hear the echo of his knock, but no one came to the door. "That's funny, I'm sure this is the right house." Finally a scrubby dog barked twice, yawned, and lay down for a nap. Turning towards his pickup he ran smack into Darla, "Hi, I was beginning to think I was at the wrong place."

12

"No, in the summer little is done in the heat of the day, it's Osage exercise time."

"What do you mean?"

"That's a joke. Osage Indians always take a nap after a big meal. So in Indian country, Osage exercise simply means to take a nap."

"Oh."

"Come here, let me look at you. I'm glad you came a little early, we will have time to talk before the powwow. There will be a lot of people here, some of our Riverside classmates will be here too. One other thing, will you be my boyfriend during the powwow? I don't have a steady, and I would like to introduce you to my kinfolks. I want to grab you before the rest of the girls get here, so that it will be hands off."

"OK. I never had a real girlfriend before."

"Why not?"

"I've been too busy. Don't think girls are off limits for me, it's just that I had so many things to do."

"There will be fringe benefits."

"Like what?"

"Well, something like this." Darla reached up and put her arms around Jake, finishing it off with a deep kiss.

"Wow! Yes I'll be your boyfriend."

Smiling Darla led Jake around to the back of the house.

"You know, I liked the fringe benefits."

"You haven't seen anything yet."

This was a heady experience for Jake, he kept remembering what his mother told him. Life seemed a little more complicated than he thought it would be. There are no free rides.

"Come on Jake, something bothering you?"

"Yes."

"Like what?"

"You."

"I didn't know I bothered you. At school you hardly looked at me. I did everything I could to attract you, you just didn't respond."

"I was kinda busy, but now I have plenty of time. So where do we start?"

"You have a room priority. I'll show you the bedroom you will use, mine is across the hall."

13

"OK."

Darla led him up a giant staircase. It was circular, constructed like those in a southern mansion. Jake was deeply impressed. On the first landing he noticed a Paul Gauguin, and at the top of the staircase was a Jean Augste Ingres, " Odalisque." "Are these originals?"

"No, they're just copies. My father said they are very good prints."

"Where did your father learn about such famous artists?"

"When he was a young man he spent several summers in Europe. He speaks very good French. He spent a year in Paris, and was a student part of the time at the Louvre. He talks about the Champs Elysees, and the boulevards with coffee shops. It was a very pleasant time for him."

"I'll bet. I envy him."

"Here's your room. You can put some of your things in the dresser. And there are hangers in the closet. We never lock doors, but I don't think anyone will rob you." Darla had a sly grin on her face. "The bath is down the hall, your towels are on the dresser. You would probably like to rest and clean up a little. "Thanks for coming." Darla put her arms around Jake and gave him a big kiss. "See you after while. If you like, we can do more of the same."

"Sounds good to me." Jake lay on the bed and reflected about his trip and the events of the day.

The summer breezes drifted into Jake's room. His breathing kept up with the tempo. His dreams almost always were about Mary Marie, she had left an impression on him.

"Hi Jake, where have you been?"

It took him a few minutes to determine if he was dreaming or was it real...he was dreaming. Jake reached out to touch her, she laughed and walked into his arms. "Mary Marie, Mary Marie, where have you been? I've missed you, I find myself daydreaming about you."

"I'm pleased because I, too, have thought of you."

"It's hard for me to explain because I've never felt this way about a girl."

"Why me?"

"I really don't know, I have been asking myself the same thing. Of course you are beautiful, friendly, an all-American girl.

It's a combination of the physical, plus a feeling I have about you. I find myself thinking about you all of the time, I want to be with you forever."

"Are you sure Jake? You have only met me one time."

"Yeah, I know. Sometimes that is all that it takes."

"When I marry, I want it to be forever. I'm a little wild, maybe crazy, but I want to live awhile before I commit myself to one man."

"You want to live around?"

"If it takes that to learn, my answer is yes."

For a moment Jake thought the dream would fade away. As he reached out for her, she became more distant. He spoke but she didn't answer, only the faint outline of her body was visable. "Mary Marie, don't leave me. I need you, I want to talk some more."

"The more you want me, the better you will be able to see me."

"Why can't I hold you in my arms?"

"I'm afraid not, that would spoil everything."

"Why?"

"Silly, because this is only a dream, if you touch me I will disappear. If you want me you will have to come to my home. I live near Hominy, Oklahoma, on the road from Cleveland."

"Man, this is some dream. I can't believe it, directions and everything."

A door slammed someplace in the house. Jake stirred, rolled over, it was becoming warm in the room. More noise. Then there was a knock on the door.

"Jake, Jake!" The door opened, it was Darla. "Are you sick? I have been knocking on the door. I could hear some mumbling noises, like someone was talking. I thought there was someone in the room with you, were you talking to a girl?"

"Well, it was a dream; there was a girl in it."

"It sounded like you enjoyed it."

"I did. It was about a girl I knew once...it doesn't really mean anything.

"Well, just put on your pants, it's time to eat."

Jake had forgotten that he had stripped down to his shorts. "Oh my God, I didn't...'"

"That's alright. I have four brothers, I'm used to men going

15

around in their underwear."

"Yes, but I'm not your brother."

"I hope not, because it wouldn't be so much fun if you were. Come on, get your pants on. I'm going down and help in the kitchen. And take that silly grin off your face!"

Jake went down the hall to the bathroom, washed his face, and combed his hair. As he went down the stairs he could hear voices and sounds from the kitchen. He walked towards the sounds, entering a large room. Everyone was seated at the table. As they glanced up Darla said, "Dad and Mother, this is Jake Hawkins."

"I'm glad to know you."

Darla went around the table calling out the names of her brothers and the guests. Darla's father said, "Come on, Jake sit down and have at it."

"Right here Jake." Darla pulled out the chair next to hers. She was dressed in a cowboy shirt, jeans, and boots. When she wasn't watching, Jake took a real good look. No doubt about it, Darla was a knockout. He wondered how come she picked him.

One of the smaller cousins came out with, "Aunt Darla, is this the guy you are going to marry?"

She came back with, "I don't know about him, but it sounds like a good idea to me."

Jake could feel his face getting red. Darla's father came to his rescue. "Leave Jake alone, he is our company. You little boys mind your manners, or there will be no powwow for you."

"Well, I was just wondering."

Darla said, "That's enough, knock it off." After that everyone sat without talking. Finally Darla broke the ice, "Jake after supper I will show you around." One of the little boys started to say something, but Darla's father gave him a sharp look.

Jake was glad when the meal was over. He started to carry his plate to the kitchen, but Darla's father said, "I see you've been well trained, but the little boys and girls will clean up the table."

"Ah Dad, we always have to do it. We wanted to watch."

"Watch what?"

"Jake and Darla."

"You guys start cleaning up, and not another word."

Stepping outside the house, Jake looked toward the west. There seemed to be miles and miles of rolling hills with cattle grazing on short grass.

"Over this way, Jake. I have two horses saddled, it's too far to walk. And the cook fixed us a picnic lunch with some apple juice. Riding always makes me hungry."

"Me too."

Jake was a good rider. He had been raised around horses and cattle, he frequently helped the neighbors at round-up time.

Darla had been raised here on her father's ranch and knew the cattle lingo. She had camped under the stars during round-up, sometimes helping with the cooking. She knew the life of a ranch, and she loved it.

Darla led off as if she knew where she wanted to go, and she did. She was headed for Coyote Springs where there was always shade. Since she was little her family had gone to the springs, it was a good place to get away from the cares of the day.

Darla slowed down. When Jake rode up beside her she asked, "How do you like the ranch?"

"It's big, I've never seen anything like this before. It's more than I expected."

"You probably thought I lived on some broken down ranch. Right?"

"No, I didn't think that. For sure, this is a fine ranch."

"Coyote Springs is right over that hill, that's where we are headed."

"Great."

"You ride very well for a tenderfoot."

"Well, I'm not exactly a tenderfoot. We don't live on a ranch, but I have ridden horses since I was small. I've helped the ranchers around home when they were shorthanded. I can see it would be a good life."

"My dad would love you for those words. He thinks only of the ranch, the cattle, and his family. He has often said his son-in-law had to be a rancher."

"Does that let me out?"

"No...I think you would probably pass the test." Darla felt the devil nudge her on, "Is that a proposal?"

"No, no, no. I can see you have much to offer, good family traditions, beauty, everything a man could want."

"But not you?"

"Darla, I have lots of things to do before I marry. I want to be able to offer a woman something that I have created on my own. I have a lot of growing up to do."

"Well, here we are. What do you think of Coyote Springs?" It was like an oasis in a desert, the cold water from the springs had created a haven away from home.

Darla dismounted, took the food out of the saddlebags, and in one motion spread a tablecloth on the ground. As if by magic, there was a plate of fried chicken, homemade bread, celery sticks, and apple juice. "Help yourself! Grab a plate, fill it up, and come sit by me."

The ride had been hot. They had kept a steady pace, covering a lot of ground. Now it was time to eat—conversation could come later.

"Man, that was good. I was really hungry."

"I'm glad. I like to see a man enjoy his food."

"I'm a growing boy."

"You don't look like any boy to me."

"What do I look like?"

"A man."

"And you like men?"

"Well, not all men. I am selective."

"How about this man?"

"I think you will pass the test. There is one thing though, I am jealous of the girl you were talking to in your dream."

"I hardly know her, as I only met her once, and that was in a dream. I don't have any deep feelings about her, but she is a beautiful Osage girl that we caught a ride with when we were hitching...in that dream."

"Who is we?"

"Robert Gombi, you know, we were classmates at Riverside."

"Yeah, I remember. Both of you spent a lot of time together. You didn't spend much time with girls."

"That was when we were in school, now we are grown up. You said I looked like a man."

"Yeah. Do you know how men are with western women?"

"Sure. We treat them with respect, and we are always ready to learn."

"Let's have a lesson. Come over here, let's see if you know how to kiss."

Under his breath Jake muttered, "I think I'm going to like this lesson." He slid his arm around Darla, kissing her lightly on the mouth, ears, neck and hair. The embrace really was the first physical expression of affection that he had shown any girl. "That was great, I'm ready for lesson number two."

"Whoa, slow down boy, let me get my breath."

Both Jake and Darla pulled back and took a long look at each other. Jake said, "You know, in my family there isn't a lot of hugging and kissing, although we care for each other. I don't know why, it just wasn't a part of our life-style."

"It's the way your parents were brought up. My mother is very affectionate, my father waits for her to make the first move. Don't let it worry you, everyone has the ability to give and receive love. It's just a matter of the way you think, I don't believe it's atavistic."

"What's that?"

"In your genes, maybe a throwback in heredity."

"What do genes have to do with loving?"

"I'm not sure, but they have a lot to do with intelligence, height, skin color. You inherit a lot of things from your parents."

"I still don't see how this affects physical attraction."

"I don't either," Darla admitted, "but I've read that we may have inherited the capacity to learn, or to do anything. You may be shy or bashful, but I still say you can learn how to love...with practice." Darla was very composed, smiling all the time she was talking to Jake. "Ready for another lesson?"

"Yes, I'm ready."

Darla rolled over on her back in the soft grass. She looked up at him. Jake was at a loss, but somehow he lay down beside her, and stroked her hair and cheeks. The scent of her perfume filled his senses. He pulled her roughly into his arms. This time he made up for lack of experience with brutal kisses.

Darla placed her hands against his chest. "Jake...let me breathe." Taking a deep breath, she stroked the back of his head and teased his ears. She could hear his heart thump, she thought it was going to run away.

This time it was Jake who pulled away, rolling over on his back, aware of only one thing—he must have Darla.

"Jake, do you want me?"

"Yes."

"Have you ever had a girl before?"

"No."

19

"I like you, Jake, more than I care to admit, but I don't want to get pregnant."

"Are you on the pill?"

"No, I'm not. I am not ready for that."

"Maybe you're not ready for love."

"Maybe. I guess I thought I was a big girl. I've got to have time to think. I'm sorry, Jake, when I sift out all of my thoughts I'll let you know. Something else...I have never had a man, so I guess we are two babes-in-the-woods. Maybe I'm scared, I've heard what happened to a lot of girls at school. They thought they were in love, got pregnant, then dropped out of school. Their boyfriends dropped them...just walked out, and the girl was left with a baby."

"Yes, I know. Maybe you're right. What do you say we go back to the house. Your father will be wondering about us."

"Jake, you aren't mad at me are you? I do like you, maybe I love you."

Both of them gathered up the remains of their picnic lunch. Jake walked over to hold her stirrup while she mounted. Darla didn't expect this, but she liked it.

Then Jake mounted his horse. "You lead off, I'll follow." Actually he wanted a little time to himself, without conversation. That was a close call. The fragrance of Darla's clothes still lingered, haunting him with the scene in the grass.

Arriving at the stable, one of the cow punchers took over their mounts. He removed the saddles and bridles, and rubbed the horses down with dry hay. They trotted away from the stable, rolled in the dust, and headed for the trough for a drink of water.

Walking slowly to the house, Jake and Darla were both aware of their feelings.

"Jake."

"Yes."

"I do love you."

"That's nice. I have strong feelings about you, too."

"Give me a little time, will you?"

"Sure, take all the time you want."

"What does that mean?"

"It means that we are not as grown-up as we thought."

"I'll call you for supper."

"OK."

20

Jake found himself in his room. He didn't remember entering the house or climbing the stairs, it was as if he were in a dream world. He walked toward the large bay window. The expanse of the plains country was unbelievable. Here and there a Hereford steer crossed his view. It all seemed so peaceful, so well organized. Why does life have to be so full of uncertainties.

His psyche nudged him, "Oh, go ahead. What the hell! It will be fun."

Jake responded, "Yeah, but what about the day after?"

"You can always walk off. You don't have anything to lose."

"But what about Darla, she has a lot to lose."

"That's tough, it's the chance she takes."

"That's what I'm afraid of."

"I believe you're chicken."

"I probably am."

"I know you are."

"I never did think I could fall in love with a woman so fast."

"That's what they all say. Sooner or later they all get bitten."

"Who bites them?"

"The love bug."

"What's the remedy?"

"There isn't any remedy, it has to wear off."

"How long does it take?"

"It depends upon the number of times you have been bitten, and how hard. You mean to tell me you have never been bitten by the love bug?"

"I was always too busy."

"Sooner or later, all men are bitten."

"All men?"

"Well, almost all. There are some men who never become interested in women."

"Why is that?"

"I don't rightly know. Some people say it's too much mother. I guess that is as good an answer as any."

"I never heard about this at school."

"You don't learn it at school boy. It comes with you. It looks to me like you have a bad case, but don't worry, you will get over it."

"Damn! I feel like packing up and leaving. I could put all this love business behind me."

Jake got down his old suitcase and put all of his things in it.

He suddenly felt very sleepy, and decided to take a short nap.

He fell asleep immediately. His breathing matched the rhythm. of the soft breezes coming through the window. This time it wasn't Mary Marie, but Darla that he dreamed about.

"God damn you, Darla. You didn't have any business making me fall in love with you."

"You didn't have to."

"If it hadn't been for you I would be on my way by now."

"Come on Jake, I won't hurt you."

"I know you won't."

"Then come over close to me."

It was so real, that when Jake reached out for Darla, he knew it wasn't a dream. She was real, she was there in body.

"What the hell are you doing in my room? If your Dad finds us here he will kill me."

Although he had been asleep, he was coming to life real fast. He saw that Darla had removed all of her clothes.

Jake jumped up as if he was shot. "Oh my God, get your clothes back on. Jesus...your father will kill me."

"He isn't here, everyone is gone. Our neighbor invited them over for supper. I told them we didn't want to go."

Jake was still in a state of shock. "Even so, someone might come back."

Darla got up, went over to the door, and locked it. "Now we won't be bothered. Take your clothes off and come lay down beside me. I'll rub your back."

Jake knew that Darla was challenging him, trying to make him a fool, a dunce. "I can't do it Darla, I love you too much. Put on your clothes, and we will go downstairs and talk."

"I'm tired of talking, I want you."

It was too much. Jake grabbed his packed suitcase and unlocked the bedroom door. Going down the staircase he hardly hit the steps. Running out to his pickup he threw in the suitcase, started the engine, and was on his way. "I'm probably the biggest dumbell that ever lived, running away from a deal like that. I just couldn't do it. I just couldn't."

His psyche spoke up again, "I know. While you are at it, you should put on your pants."

Jake pulled over and stopped the pickup with a screech. He didn't want to go back for his clothes. He opened his suitcase and

22

found a pair of jeans.

Jake hardly saw the road on the way home, the entire trip was made in a daze. Pulling into his yard he noticed that all of the cars were gone. "Thank God," he thought, "I won't have to talk to anyone. I've got to keep on moving, there will be too many questions."

Jake knew he would need more money; he had a small checking account in the Anadarko Bank and Trust. His mother had washed and ironed his clothes, so he grabbed another pair of jeans along with his favorite cowboy shirt. He stopped long enough to write himself a check and his parents a note.

Dear Father and Mother:
I'm off to Hominy, Oklahoma to visit some
friends. I will call after I arrive.

Love,
Jake

2

Hominy wasn't the easiest place in the world to get to. Checking his map he planned to go north on I-35 to Perry, east to Cleveland, then ten miles northeast to Hominy. It was about a three hour trip, give or take a little. Then he would have to find Mary Marie Tinker. It was a long shot...he hoped it would pay off.

When he got to Cleveland he pulled in at a gas station. Two men were in a heated argument. It sounded like politics, every once in a while he heard the names Reagan and Kennedy.

This went on for about five minutes, when one of the men came over to him. "Who are you voting for?"

"Me?"

"Yes, you."

"I didn't know there was an election."

"There isn't, but if there was, who would you vote for?"

"Well, I'm a Democrat."

"See, I told you Kennedy would win!"

Then the other man said, 'That don't mean anything. I bet that boy isn't old enough to vote. How old are you, boy?"

"Eighteen."

"See, he isn't old enough."

Jake was getting impatient. 'Say, could I buy some gas?"

"You're dern tootin', you can buy all of the gas you want since you're a Democrat. If you was a Republican I wouldn't sell you any. But you could get some gas over at the Texaco station. He's a Republican, they sell to anyone."

"Can either one of you men tell me where a girl by the name

24

of Mary Marie Tinker lives?''

That stopped them. "You mean that wild, Osage girl?''

"Well, I don't know about her habits, I just want to know where she lives.''

The owner of the Gulf station turned and pointed, "See that road yonder?''

"Yes.''

"Well, you take that one, and follow it for about ten miles, and you will run right by her house. It's the only one along there, and it's a big one. Are you kin to Miss Tinker?''

"No, I'm just a friend.''

"Just wondering. I'd be careful if I was you. I hear there are lots of wild parties at that place, not a fit place for a decent boy. You like hookers?''

"No, do you?''

"Don't get smart with me, boy. I was just trying to be friendly.''

"Thanks for the information.''

Hookers. Funny the old man asked him such a question. He's probably just some crazy white man. Wonder what makes them so nosey.

The road between Cleveland and Hominy was blacktop, but it was full of chuckholes. Jake had to be alert so he wouldn't break a spring. On both sides of the road were large elm trees, their branches met and formed a cover.

Jake had been on the road since midday. In the excitement he had forgotten to eat, now he was hungry. First he had to see if Mary Marie was at home. He kept a sharp lookout for the house. That could be it, the two men said it was the only one along this road.

There was a slight jog in the road, on his right a large clapboard house loomed. In the yard was an American flag, below it was another flag that Jake didn't recognize. Turning into the drive he was surprised to see rose bushes along one side. In a way, it reminded him of the large plantation houses he had seen in the south. It was a combination of colonial, western, New England and Indian. The front of the house reminded him of the White House in Washington, D.C. There were columns placed at regular intervals, forming an Italian colonade. It was very striking.

Jake pulled his pickup over to the curb. He walked to the door and rang the bell. Finally, after a long wait, a black man answered the door. "Yes, sir?"

"I'm looking for Mary Marie Tinker."

"Do you know her?"

"Yes, she wanted me to visit her."

The old man mumbled something about her inviting everyone she knows. "She's out in back, taking a sunbath by the pool. You go aroung yonder, you can't miss it."

Jake couldn't get over the place, so well designed and landscaped. It was really something.

Following the directions of the servant, he went along the brick path to the back of the house. French doors opened on an expanse of courtyard paved with bricks. Sloping off from this he could see the pool. It sparkled like a blue diamond. It was lined with an assortment of umbrellas and chaise lounges.

Mary Marie was lying under one of the umbrellas and seemed to be asleep. She was wearing a string bikini and a top. There was just enough noise from his walk down to the pool to awaken her. "Hi, Who are you?"

"I'm Jake Hawkins. I met you in a dream."

"A dream?"

"It's a long story, but to make a long story short, while I was at school I dreamed about an Osage girl named Mary Marie Tinker."

"Come on, you expect me to believe that?"

"Believe it or not, that's why I'm here. It probably was ESP."

"That's a tall tale! But I'm glad you came, get yourself something to drink at the bar."

"It's kinda early to drink."

"It's never too early to drink. Always comes in handy."

Jake mumbled, "She's just as beautiful as I thought she'd be."

"What did you say?"

"I said, you are beautiful."

"Oh that, I get tired of people telling me that."

"You also have a beautiful home."

"Yes, and that too."

"It's unbelieveable."

"You can do anything if you have the money."

"Well, almost anything," mused Jake.

"Sometimes money hurts more than it helps. The white

26

people around here are very jealous of the rich Osages, they do everything to make their lives miserable."

"You don't look miserable to me."

"No, I have learned to live with red-necks."

"Do you live here without relatives or friends?"

"This place was built by my father. He was educated in the east, he also spent considerable time in Europe. When the Osages came into all the money, it gave him a chance to put some of his ideas to work. Everything is European, except that brush arbor over there.

"He thought having this place would give him status in town. Well...it didn't. Behind his back they called it 'Tinker's Folly', or that 'European Ghost House'. That kinda killed his spirit. It got so bad that he hardly went into the house."

"What about the arbor?"

"Father had that constructed after he got sick of the house.

"He had some Kiowas from Mountain View come up and make it. After it was completed he spent the rest of his life living there, that is, when he was here."

"What about your mother?"

Mary Marie looked out into space, she didn't say anything for a long time. "My mother...well, let me tell you about my mother. My father met her out east, I guess while he was in school. He was crazy in love with her. She was a real lady, a blue blood. She was related to the Mellons of Pittsburg, old Andrew himself. I heard they almost died when she married my father, because he was an Indian, a savage from out west.

"He built this house for her. She knew all the fine arts of entertaining. She hired big bands from Kansas City to come here." Again Mary Marie looked out into the blue expance, and watched the drifting clouds. "Mother gave her parties, and invited the people around here to come and see. No one came but some broken-down politicians and poor white trash. She tried two or three times, with the same results." Again, Mary Marie hesitated. Jake noticed that she was crying. "It broke their spirits and their hearts.

"Mother stayed on until after I was born, then she went back east. Of course, I went with her. I was never accepted by my kinfolks. They looked at me like I was something out of a zoo. As soon as I was old enough, I called my dad and told him I wanted to come home. I wanted to live in Indian country.

"The medical records show that my father died of a heart attack, actually it was a broken heart. He's buried over on that hill, he always said he wanted to be buried on the biggest hill around. I hope he is sleeping peacefully now."

"And your mother?"

"I made peace with my mother some time ago. After she left with me she never came back. They never did get a divorce, they were still in love. They married before their time and the world wasn't ready for it. God damn it to hell! Why am I telling you all of this?"

"I'm glad you did, it's really a very sad but beautiful story."

"What makes me so crazy is that I inherited all my father's money, and my mother left me another fortune. So here I am, a no-good Osage, at least that's what the white people say."

"Do you ever go back to Pittsburg to see the Mellons?"

"Yes, and no. They handle most of my money affairs, so I go back about once a year. Charles Mellon is the only one that I like.

"Enough talk!" Pulling off her bikini she walked over to the pool, diving in with grace and ease. "Come on in. You don't need a suit, there is no one here except us."

What the hell, if she can do it, I can too. So, peeling off everything, he dove in.

"Want to race?" shouted Mary Marie.

"Sure!"

"Alright, the loser has to mix the drinks."

"You drink too much."

"I know, it keeps me from thinking."

The swimming and horseplay went on for awhile. Mary Marie was the first to get out. She went to the nearest chair, grabbed a towel, and dried off. Jake did the same, as it seemed like a good idea.

"What did they tell you about me in town?"

"How did you know I stopped?"

"I didn't, I just guessed that you did."

"You really want to know?"

"Yes."

"They said you were a hooker."

At that Mary Marie screamed with delight, "You see, my white

28

friends are still at it! Hooker, huh? Well, that's one profession I don't have to follow. I might make love with a man if I liked him, but not for money..." Mary Marie looked straight at Jake. "Have you ever made love?"

"No."

"Well, at least you're honest. Most men brag about all of the lay jobs they've had. You know, I hope you are real. I haven't met a real man, although I keep looking. Tell me about yourself."

"Where do you want me to start."

"Wherever you want."

"I am the son of an Indian preacher. My mother, like yours, is white. My dad is well educated, and so is my mother."

Jake stopped. Looking out on the hilly country, he said quietly, "It's nice here."

"I think my dad is disappointed that he hasn't moved up the ladder, his churches have been small, rural ones. My mother came from successful farm people in western Kansas. They met in a small college, fell in love, and married. My mother supports my dad in everything he does. I think she would like to move close to her folks, but she won't put any pressure on my dad to move."

"Your folks seem like nice people."

"They are that. Looking back on my life, I think they really wanted me."

"No hang-ups?"

"None that I know of."

"You're lucky. Money doesn't buy happiness."

"In a way I'm very lucky. Since my dad's churches have been in small towns, I am, I suppose, a country boy. I remember a lot of good times swimming in the Washita River in the hot, lazy, summer days. We would stay in all day, then go home and eat evrything in sight. Boys and girls swam in the same place. We didn't have swimsuits, didn't think anything of it. We were all just kids, in the era before the crazies.

"We were raised around animals. I think today's kids are cheated. They don't have wide, open spaces to move around in. Everything is packaged, they don't know how to made-do."

There was a long pause, finally Mary Marie grabbed Jake's hand. "Come on, let's go to the house. We should be able to find something to eat."

"An Indian steak sandwich?" suggested Jake.

29

"What's Indian steak?"

"Bologna, only the Indians call it Indian steak."

"Why do they like this special sandwich?"

"They don't like it for the taste, they like it because it's cheap and will fill them up. They would rather have steak."

"Well, I guess I don't know much about Indians, although I'm half Osage. A lot of white people think Indians are all alike. They don't know that each tribe has its own culture and language. I don't believe the Osage tribe falls into the Plains Indian group. I think they moved to Indian Territory from the region between the Missouri and Arkansas Rivers."

Walking hand in hand to the house, they brushed their bodies against each other. Jake felt a current of electricity run through his body. He was getting light-headed, possibly because he was hungry, or because of Mary Marie.

As they neared the rear entrance Jake noticed the black servant in the yard. "Is there anything I can do for you, Miss Tinker?"

"No, thanks. We'll just make some sandwiches."

"Is it alright if I leave early? My wife is doing poorly, and I want to see about her?"

"It's alright, you may go. I hope your wife feels better."

Mary Marie made some cold chicken sandwiches and opened two cans of beer.

"This is such a big house, do you live here alone? Oh, I'm sorry, that really isn't any of my business."

"That's alright. Yes, I live here alone most of the time. Then I get bored, and drive or fly someplace else to break the monotony."

"I never had that trouble. Seems like I have always had more than my share of things to do."

"You're fortunate. I can tell you don't seem to be as restless as most of the people I know."

After a long pause Jake said, "I know you don't like to be told you are beautiful, but you are one of the most beautiful girls I have met."

"Are you sure it isn't the beer talking?"

"I don't think so. It makes it easier, I guess."

30

When they finished their lunch Mary Marie said, "Just leave the mess, my servant will be back in the morning. Come on with me, I've got something I want to show you."

Again Mary Marie took his hand, "It's this way." They hurried up the staircase under a sparkling chandelier which gave even more beauty to the house. A soft breeze was coming down a long, carpeted hall. "Here it is, my bedroom."

"It's beautiful." The room was carpeted in snow-white, and there was an enormous king-size bed.

Mary Marie took off her blouse and shorts, she wore only a bikini. "It's alright, take off your clothes, there isn't anyone in the house." She sat in a chaise lounge. "Draw up a chair, I want to talk. A while ago you mentioned the hot, summer days in Anadarko, and some of things you used to do—tell me more."

"Well, summertime around Anadarko is powwow time. All of the Plains Indians are good dancers. Everybody takes part, children too. What I like most is the music, Plains Indian music has a lot of rhythm. I like to hear the drums and the high-pitched notes that the womenfolks do.

"The entire celebration is a social event. There is always some drinking, young bucks and their girls have to try booze. And there is some grass smoked, but not a lot. Overall, the Plains Indian culture is well defined, maybe not as much as some tribes in the west, but it's what holds them together."

"That's very interesting. I wish I knew as much about Indians as you do."

"The Indian way to learn is by association. They will be skeptical at first, but after they find out that you are sincere they will open up."

"What's a powwow baby?"

Jake thought she knew the answer before she asked the question—typical of Indians—she was probably more Indian than she realized. "A lot of young people at a powwow get on an emotional high, plus too much beer. Some girls just want to experiment with boys. If a girl has a baby, not too much is said, unless she belongs to a leading family in the community." Jake felt he had said enough, and really wanted to hear more about Mary Marie. "I know you told me a lot about yourself, but I'm sure there's more."

"Yes, there is a lot more, only most of it is show."

"What do you mean, show?"

"A lot of my drinking is an effort to cover up. I have been very lonely. I love this house, because it was my mother's and father's home, and because my father is buried close by. But it gets lonely, I don't have any close friends."

"How about me?"

"Thank you, I hope you are my friend, and that you will stay here for a while. I have a feeling I could love you. In a way you remind me of my father. I suppose a girl often chases a man that has her father's traits."

"Yes, she probably does."

"You remember those white men calling me a hooker? Well, I've done a lot of things I'm not proud of, but I've never slept around. I've been propositioned often enough, but none of the men had what I wanted. It's true I have put away a lot of booze, mostly to drive away the lonliness. My parents have been gone several years, but I still miss them."

"I'm glad to hear you say you miss them, you must have had very strong ties."

Jake got up and walked to the window. Suddenly he turned to face her and said, "It's none of my business, but have you ever lived with a man?"

"Hell no, I haven't met the man I want. You know, I haven't talked to anyone the way I have to you, you just naturally fit. Will you stay here for a while?"

"I can't stay too long because I've made some other plans."

"You don't like it here?"

"I love it here. You are beautiful, your home is beautiful. I wish I had known your mother and father."

"I do too. Jake, come over here and hold me close, I want to be near you. Don't say anything, just hold me."

Jake picked her up and carried her to the large window looking out to the west. "Isn't it beautiful?"

"Yes, it is. Nature is beautiful, but it can also be very destructive. I remember some of the spring storms here...wind...lightning. Alone in this big house it can be a little frightening."

"I think you are very strong to do it."

"That's where the booze comes in, if I'm about half loaded, I don't care. I can sleep through it all."

"I understand. I don't know if I could live here alone for

any length of time, it would be very difficult. You know, you need people."

"You are very wise."

"No, I'm really just a country boy."

"I wouldn't say that. You are young in years, but you know a lot."

"Yes, I know a lot about horses and beef cattle. But when it comes to girls I'm afraid I am very green."

"Don't worry, you have all the equipment. I don't think you will have any problems."

Jake said, "You look worried. What's the matter?"

"You remember those white men who called me a hooker? I told you the white people around here would say anything about an Indian. Especially an Indian woman, because they know they can get away with it."

"Why don't you sue them?"

"It wouldn't hold up. I wouldn't have a chance."

"Why not?"

"Not with a non-Indian jury. I could get some Indians to testify, but the white attorney would tear them to pieces. I will just have to ride it out."

"Someday Indians are going to use the courts to their advantage."

"Yes, but not me."

"You have the money to put up a good fight."

"I guess I don't have the guts for it."

"We need everyone's help."

"What are you, some kind of preacher?"

"No, but my father is. He believes in using the courts. But life is full of fears and worries, there is always something holding people back. It's easy to talk about what someone else should do. When it comes to the doing, that's another thing. Well, we have become very wise, poor men's philosophers."

"Now back to that question...do you think I'm a hooker?"

Jake didn't say anything for a long time. "Does that put me in the same category as the white men?"

"No, but there was some doubt in your mind. I am not a virgin, but I don't sleep around. I'm waiting for a special man. It could be you. How long can you stay as my guest?"

"First I have to call my folks, I told them I would as soon as

33

I arrived.''

"It must be nice to have someone who cares."

"It has always been that way, we are a very close family. Both of my parents are wise, and they answer all my questions easily.''

"Questions about girls?''

"I don't think either of them would be surprised if I had a sexual experience. They probably feel that they have raised me as best they could. My mother is very wise in the ways of women. I'm sure they hope I will get an education and marry someday.''

"Well, you had better make that call. The phone is across the hall.''

Jake made the call and returned to Mary Marie's room. In his absence she had removed all of her clothes, and was lying on the big bed. "Come on Jake, I want you. Take your clothes off, love me. I want you.''

Jake was so nervous he couldn't get his clothes off.

"Come over here, I'll help you.''

The closeness of Mary Marie, the perfume she had used, intoxicated him. Her body was beautiful.

Mary Marie helped him with his clothes. It was exciting to her. Most of the men she knew wanted her so badly they were brutal, it was wonderful to be loved.

From that moment on through the rest of the afternoon, there was a series of loving, kissing, holding each other meshed as one. They experienced the whole spectrum of human emotion, from intense bliss to desolate despair, despair that their loving could not go on forever. For Jake it was an incredibly potent experience. For Mary Marie it was beautiful, she felt so very close to Jake. It was as if she were in another world, a very beautiful world. Mary Marie didn't realize that she was sexually hungry, not solely for release, but a blissful union with a very special man. She was very happy.

The days drifted on like a dream. They would swim, lay in the sun and talk. When hungry they would go up to the kitchen and find something in the refrigerator. On occasion, the black servant, Gustavo, would bring down a tray of food. In the evening they would drive to Hominy to get supplies, and check the post office box. They would swim and talk some more, then go to Mary Marie's room where they would spend the rest of the night. One evening the phone rang, it was for Jake. It was Robert Gombi.

"Hey, man, when are you coming home? You know we have things to do this summer."

"How did you get this number?"

"From your mother, she said you would be back in a week."

"I might stay on."

"What?"

"I said I might stay on."

"Hey, lover boy, don't get too deep. Many a man has been trapped by a set of big, brown eyes, or something."

"Yeah, or something."

"I'm serious, this is your old friend Robert talking. We have things to do."

There was a long pause, then Jake asked, "What is today?"

"Thursday. Damn, you are really gone."

"I'll tell you what, I will be home Monday?"

"Which Monday?"

"The next one."

"You want to know something?"

"No."

"Well, I'm going to tell you anyway. I think your parents are worried."

"Yes?"

"Yes."

"OK, and thanks. I'll be shoving off Monday." Jake promised.

"Tell me something, Jake."

"OK."

"What is it with this lover boy bit."

"Shut up. I can handle it."

"Alright, alright. I was just asking. Man, you really have changed."

"See ya later."

"Bye."

When Jake returned to Mary Marie's room she was dressed in a western shirt, jeans and boots. "I'm tired of the house. I need some fresh air."

"You want to walk?"

"No, I want to ride." While Jake was on the phone, Mary Marie had asked the servant to bring her Porche around. It was a very sporty roadster, custom-made for her.

"Crawl in, I want to drive. I need some excitement."

Jake enjoyed excitement, but he remembered her driving in his dream. Mary Marie gunned the Porche down the blacktop road, faster and faster til it felt like they were flying.

"If we meet someone it will be head-on. I hope to hell everyone stays home this evening," yelled Jake.

At the edge of Cleveland Mary Marie slowed down a little. Jake saw the filling station where he had stopped, fortunately there was no one in sight. She drove through the arch of the station, barely missing a pump. She knocked over a can of bottle caps, and sent an old, red chicken flying. The station operator could be seen hollering, shaking his fist. "God-damned, crazy Osage!"

"That's for calling me a hooker, you son of a bitch. The next time, I'll run over your ass."

Jake saw the Gulf station operator come across the street. "Want me to call the law?"

"No use to call them, they couldn't catch the clap on their way home. I'm going to get me a double-barreled shotgun and get me an Osage."

"Cool down, that's nothing but trouble."

Mary Marie pulled in at a convenience store where she got a pack of beer. "Open this, will you Jake? I want a drink."

Jake reached over to Mary Marie, "Not now, wait till we get home."

"Why wait? The red-neck cops can't catch me?"

"And if they do?"

"They have all tried to get me in bed with them, they won't do anything."

"Might be the state patrol," warned Jake.

"Yes, it might. Let's get the hell out of here."

When they entered the house they could hear the phone ringing. Jake reached the phone first, "Hello."

"Jake?"

"Yes."

"I think you had better come home." Jake noticed that his mother's voice was shaky.

"What's wrong, Mother?"

"Your father has had a heart attack."

"I'll be there," said Jake, and he hung up.

36

"Anything wrong?"

"Yes My father has had a heart attack. My mother needs me."

"I'm sorry."

"Thanks."

Jake got his things together and took off down the road.

Jake was in a daze. Past events flashed through his mind. He blamed himself for not spending more time with his father. He felt he had been selfish and should have helped out more at home. He had been a part of a religious family for so long that guilt tugged at his mind. He decided that his affair with Mary Marie may have triggered his father's heart attack. "And the God damned white churches, they wouldn't give my dad a chance."

Suddenly he slowed down; "I'd better pay attention to what I'm doing, I'll run off the road and kill myself. That would be a lot of help." Most of the time he had exceeded the speed limit. He turned on his C.B. radio and listened to station 19. Truckers always watched out for "bears", and gave a reading by road markers. Jake had noticed that truckers also watched out for each other. When they hit the outskirts of Oklahoma City, some of them became lost, and the air was filled with directions. There were more and more women truck drivers. To most of them driving was a serious business, but they used such handles as Long Legs, California Rose, Arizona Sue. Jake heard a trucker with a definite regional twang talking to Sweetheart.

It seemed to Jake that the trip would never end, but finally he pulled into the yard. With screeching brakes he parked his car in his spot under the blackjack tree. His mother was waiting for him on the porch.

"How's Dad?"

"He's better."

"Where is he?"

"I admitted him to the Anadarko Hospital. The doctor said Dad would have to ease off with his work, but said he'd be alright. He said we could all help by spending more time together as a family."

"I'm sorry, Mom, I guess I've been selfish."

"Your father has been offered a church near my home in Kansas. I think some of the board members remembered that

Kansas was my home."

"I'm glad, I think we all need a change. Are you sure Dad's going to be alright?"

"That's what the doctor said. Well, how was your trip, Jake? Did you get to see the girl?"

"Yes, I saw her."

"I don't want to pry, but how did everything turn out?"

"You know me like a book, don't you."

"Not exactly."

"Mary Marie is one of the most beautiful girls I have ever seen, she is also a very unusual girl. She lives in a mansion outside of Hominy. Her father built it for her mother."

"That's nice."

"It's an incredible place. It looked like a palace to an old country boy like me. Both of her parents are dead."

"Oh, I'm sorry."

"Do you want to hear everything?"

"Not unless you want to tell me. Everyone has their own secrets and they must remain that way."

Bit by bit, Jake told his mother everything that had happened. "Are you disappointed in me?"

"First of all, you are my son and I love you. Right or wrong I love you, and will until the day I die. For now, I think it is better not to tell your father. He needs to be free of stress, perhaps later. One more thing, do you love Mary Marie?"

Jake didn't answer right away. "As I said, she's the most beautiful girl I have ever known. I am in love with her beautiful body. She has had such terrible experiences that I want to reach out to help her, to touch her, hold her, to make love to her."

Jake's mother didn't bat an eye. "I understand, I'm glad you met Mary Marie. It will be difficult to get her out of your mind."

"She has a lot going for her. Mom, she is worth over a million dollars in her own right. I don't know if I could handle that. But the thing I want to do now is to see Dad. Then, as soon as he is able, pack up and go to that church in Kansas. Oh, and one other thing. I'm hungry!"

His mother chuckled, just like a man, always hungry. Secretly, she was happy Jake was home, she leaned on him more than he knew. She wondered if Mary Marie was as beautiful as he thought. Man like, he had to find out about women.

Hurridly, she prepared some food. "It's ready, eat up."

"Don't worry, I will." Not much was said during his meal. "Man, that was good. You're the best cook in the world."

"As good as Mary Marie?"

"Well, almost."

"From now on you can get her to cook for you."

"Ah, Mom, I was teasing. You are the best."

"I know. Jake, I'm so glad you're home. I feel better already."

"I feel good too, but suddenly I'm tired. I'm going to shower and take some Osage exercise."

"What's that?"

"That's Indian for, a nap."

"You probably need it." Jake's mother poured herself a cup of coffee and picked up a piece of toast with some marmalade. She pushed open the screen door that led to the patio. The previous mission worker had been a jack-of-all-trades. He had carefully set a pattern of stones to form the patio. This was a favorite spot for her as it was shaded by a big blackjack tree.

Ruth Hawkins felt like a puppet. Someone else pulled the strings that made her dance. There were times when she doubted her ability to be a minister's wife. All her life had been spent in serving and helping, but today there was something missing. The juices of life was flowing, but there wasn't anyone to give them to. All I need is a lot of loving with a long night in bed. It would be so wonderful, like when we were first married. I couldn't get enough of my husband and he couldn't get enough of me. Ruth usually wasn't much of a dreamer, she felt it was a waste of time. But today was different—she needed it.

Ruth didn't spend much time under the blackjack tree. "I've got things to do, and here I sit mooning around like a sixteen year old girl." First she was going to the hospital, she needed to be reassured about her husband's health. She looked into Jake's room; he was still sleeping, so he could go see his father later. In a very short time she was dressed and on the road to the hospital. "Dear God, make him well. He is one of your special angels."

Ruth was aware that she was in a different mood. Something had been settled in her mind which brought on a feeling of ʾxultation. Glancing in the car mirror, she hardly recognized ʾrself—she looked younger. Parking her car, walking into the

39

hospital was almost pleasant. Before, she had been heavy of heart, today she could whip the world.

Walking into Jacob's room she saw that he was propped up in bed. He looked rested. "Hi, darling, you look like you are ready to go home." Stooping, she gave him a very warm kiss. "I'll be glad when you get out of here. I will cook you favorite supper, with all my love."

Jacob secretly liked this attention. He knew his shortcomings, he was never comfortable talking about love or showing affection. He liked it, but he always held back. "Thanks Ruth, you are a very special lady. I have been so wrapped up in my work that I have neglected you."

"Don't worry, that's behind us. First you are to get out of the hospital, rest up a little, then we are going to take a much needed vacation."

"I thought we were going to move."

"We are, but our first priority is you and a vacation. You are going to see a lot of me."

"That will be nice, I couldn't think of anything nicer. We have a lot of catching up to do."

When Jake lay down for a nap he was so exhausted that he had slept soundly. Slowly, slowly he opened his eyes, blinking at the bright sunlight filtering through the blinds. His mind was fuzzy, at first he didn't know where he was. It began to dawn on him that he was in his own room. Still, the day and the hour were blank. Hearing the door slam, he got up. Looking down the hall he could see that it was his mother. He went to the bathroom, showered, and changed into clean clothes that his mother had laid out before she left.

Jake went to the kitchen. He needed something to eat, but most of all he needed some coffee. He almost bumped into his mother.

"Hi, sleepyhead."

"Hi. You look like the cat that ate the canary."

"That's the way I feel. Your father is getting along very well, and the doctor said he could get out of the hospital very soon, and..."

"And what?"

40

"The two of us are going to take a real vacation. I have some money that my grandmother left me, we are going to use some of it."

"You think he will use your money?"

"Yes, I think he will. There are going to be some changes around here."

"What do you mean?"

"I'm not going to take over, but I am going to have a little more input about our lives."

Jake just smiled, "Is that you talking or your grandmother? As I remember, she was set in her ways."

"A little of both. I think Jacob will have more time for himself if I help him."

Jake could see that his mother had changed, she looked almost radiant, bride-like. She hummed a tune while she was fixing their meal.

"Mother, I believe you are in love."

"I am. When your father gets home there are going to be some changes made."

Jake wanted to tease his mother, but thought he had better let sleeping dogs lie. There was very little conversation during the meal, both Jake and his mother were deep in their own private thoughts. After supper his mother said, "Why don't you go to see your father now, he'll want to see you."

"Does he know about the plans for a new life?"

"Yes, I think he knows. I didn't spell it out, but he knows."

After the dishes were washed Jake was out the door before his mother knew it, "I'll see you, Mother."

"It's Mother now, not Mom." Ruth was very happy. Her husband was going to be well again, her son was no longer a boy, he was a man.

Jacob didn't remember the events leading up to his heart attack. He could faintly remember being out in the yard when he suddenly felt sick, everything was foggy, then darkness engulfed him. Gradually forms and colors became real again, and he was aware that Ruth was in the room. There was a tube attached to his nose. He thought he must be drugged, all he wanted to do was sleep. He would open his eyes, look around for awhile, then doze off again. There wasn't any rhyme or reason to his dreams.

At one point he was back in college. Those were the days, happy days. He loved competition both in the classroom and on the track field. Students he had known were in these dreams, people he hadn't thought of in years. There was a little blond that he had dated. She was walking with her million-dollar smile. Jacob reached out to touch her and she reached out to him. What was her name? It didn't matter, before he had completed his thoughts she was gone.

Now he was in the graduation procession. Thump, thump, the band was playing the usual graduation march, **Pomp and Circumstance.** He could see his family as he walked across the stage. Soon it was over. The crowd surged around the graduates, parents hugging their sons or daughters, girlfriends smiling, dreaming of things to come. Like the rest of the graduates, Jacob was glad and sad, the years at college had been wonderful. He was anxious to get out, he wanted to get started.

When he awakened from his dream, Ruth was sitting in a chair reading, "Ruth...Ruth?"

Ruth was alert to her husband's call. She bent over his bed and kissed him lightly on the cheek. "What is it, Jacob? The doctor said you were to get all of the rest possible."

"I'm getting tired of resting, I have things to do."

Ruth smiled, "Yes, I know, as soon as you get out of here we have many things to do."

"Like what?"

"That's a secret."

"I don't like secrets."

"This will have to keep until you are out of here."

Jacob was drifting again. He couldn't place where he was. Apparently he was being interviewed for a job.

"Are you an Indian?"

"Yes."

"What tribe?"

"Kiowa."

"Are you full blood?"

"No."

Silence. Jacob tried his best to remember what the interview

42

was about.

Before his mind cleared, he was back in a small, rural church preaching. He tried as hard as he could to keep things in focus.

Then he was sitting high up in a grandstand. He knew it was the American Indian Exposition because the crowd was mostly Indian. People were standing and shouting, "Come on, come on! I think I have picked a winner!" The crowd had gone wild. Now he could see horses coming around the bend.

It was night. He was still sitting in the grandstand. The crowd was gone, and all of the lights had been extinguished. Only the whispering wind was a part of him.

"How in the hell did I get here? Where is everyone?" Jacob looked around, there was no one near. He tried to stand, something was holding his arm. Finally he heard voices in the background: "I think we had better give him another shot, he seems so restless."

"Wait, call the doctor first."

"OK."

More floating. It appeared to be a church group in the east, their speech was clipped. He was standing in front of a large group of well-dressed people, his lecture notes were on the podium. The topic of his lecture was fuzzy, it must have been about Native Americans. His church often sent him to the east coast to help raise funds for the church.

"Did the Indian men all have several wives?"

"Only if they needed them."

"I don't understand...needed them?"

"It is important to remember that all Indian cultures are different. Among the Plains Indians, which was a mobile culture, each wife had a special assignment; one cooked, one set up the teepee, another searched for food, one helped tan the hides."

"Didn't the men work?"

"Oh yes, they worked very hard. Their job in this culture was to protect the family, to find food, to fight. Some Indian tribes got along very well, others were constantly at war with their enemies."

"Why did Indian tribes fight each other?"

"The best example I can think of is Europe, one country is constantly at odds with, or fighting, another. The Middle East has a record of violence."

"Yes, but that's different."

"Actually, it isn't. All of the people of the Middle Eastern countries are semetic but with different religions, each is sure it is right. Basically their cultures are different, so they fight. The Native American isn't so different, they fight other tribes because they are sure they are right and their enemy is wrong."

"Well, I don't know."

"Any other questions?"

"Why don't the Indians discard their heathen ways and become Christians and dress like us?"

"First of all, most Indians had, or have, their own religion. Some of them are Christians, as I am. On the whole they think their religion works for them. Now, most Indians wear some form of western dress. They only wear their Indian costumes when there is a dance or special occasion."

"I saw in the movies some Indians scalping a white woman."

"You can't believe what you see in the movies. The typical western is pretty much the same, the covered wagon, shooting Indians circling the wagon. Scalping was invented by the white man."

The audience gasped. "I don't think a white man could do that."

"It's a historical fact."

There was much mumbling and whispering in the audience.

"Did you ever scalp a white man?"

"No." Jacob admitted to himself that he sometimes felt like it. "I believe the best answer to any question is to go to the source. I would suggest you spend some time at one of our missions. I believe you would come away informed."

Jacob struggled to regain control of his senses. About the time he thought he was awake, he heard voices in the background, felt a slight sting...floated again.

"Eeeee, dew neh loh moh, Hong Kong, the pearl of the orient." At one point Jacob had become restless and hitchhiked to New Orleans. He signed on a fruit freighter for a year. As the ship entered the harbor there was a constant toot, toot of the various freighters. The Chinese junks didn't pay any attention. This was their harbor, the white barbarians could take a big jump. Dew neh lok moh on all of them. May the gods blow ill wind on their return trip.

This was Jacob's first trip to the orient. Hong Kong was the place he most wanted to see. Permission was granted to leave the ship. He carried a small bag for a night's stay, if he liked it he might stay two nights.

He cleared the customs dock and walked into a maze of chattering merchants. He didn't understand them, but he knew they were trying to sell him some of their wares.

A British officer was listening to an argument. He had called for a Chinese back-up, but the dialect was different, it was cantonese. He called for another, but the same thing happened.

A young Eurasian girl stopped and asked, "Officer, can I be of assistance?"

"I hope so."

The girl went into the dialect that got their attention. She brought them over to the officer and sent them on their way mumbling to themselves, "Foreign devils, foreign devils."

"Thanks, young lady. Where did you learn English?"

"Oh, I graduated from UCLA, I returned home last week."

"My thanks to you, Lady, where can I get a cab?"

"Which way are you going?"

"To the Majestic Hotel."

"It's right on my way, I'll drop you off. I'm going to Macoa."

"Is that part of Portugal?"

"Yes, it is. Macoa is small, it covers about six square miles. It's an enclave, a peninsula and two small islands at the mouth of the Canton River in China. Portugal granted broad autonomy in 1976. Great Britain says it has a population of about 500,000. Actually, I think it is much more. Do I sound like a tour guide?"

"No, I'm glad to learn something about this fascinating land."

"It is that. It's an entirely different world from that of the states."

Jacob could hear voices in his room. Through the maze of shots to make him sleep and rest he fought hard to keep in control.

Then he heard the voices of his former classmates and staff members at Riverside School. It was like walking back in time; the familiar red brick buildings, the drill teams, the inspections. In his dream he walked up to a former student. He couldn't remember his name, yet he was so very familiar. "What time is it?"

"It's 7:30."

"Morning or evening?"

"Morning, of course. You had better get on your uniform or you will get some demerits and be restricted."

"One question. What year is it?"

"What year is it?" the student repeated. "What's the matter with you? It's September 7, 1916." The student looked at him so funny that he was afraid to ask any more questions.

Jacob walked toward the boy's dormitory. On the steps he met the matron who was dressed in a long skirt and a very lacey blouse. Her hair was in braids around her head. She wore very small glasss and no makeup. "Hello, Jacob."

"Miss Drew."

"Where have you been? I haven't seen you in a long time."

"I've been on leave. Miss Drew, I want to ask you a question."

"Yes."

"Do things around Riverside seem a little old-fashioned?"

"No, I haven't noticed anything especially different. I guess you know that after the first of the year we are going to have electricity."

Jacob was stunned. How could these people not know that the world has changed.

"Miss Drew."

"Yes?"

"One more question. What day and year is this?"

"Are you joking?"

"No ma'am, I'm serious."

Smiling she said, "It's September 7, 1916. Jacob, if you don't feel well perhaps you should lie down."

"I feel alright, it's just that I can't believe what's happening."

"Dr. Chambers will be here this afternoon, perhaps you should see him."

"No, I'm alright."

The campus was familiar, and yet it was strange.

Struggling didn't help. It was Jacob's nature to overcome any obstacle, but the drugs were too much. Morphine put him in a semi-restless sleep, it also had the effect of knocking him out.

He heard the dripping rain, the low rumble of thunder. To his left the Long Toms continuously shattered the night. Under the low ceiling the noise came back, and the ground carried the vibration of the big guns. Their company had been here since October. Germans were on top of the mountain where they could see any troop movement; you could move at night, that's all.

Day after day fresh troops went up the mountain; para-troopers, the special brigade, the Polish. They had all tried to reach the top, none had succeeded. The Corps of Engineers was detailed to carry the dead back to base. Dead GI's were draped over donkeys, later they were put on jeeps for the rest of the trip back to Corps, then to the Army. It was their last ride through the chill dampness of northern Italy.

This went on day after day. Jacob never did get use to it. One day they were so full of life, with dreams of home, the next day they were on that long, last ride home. "Damn this war to hell!"

C.O. was his best friend and bunkmate. He said, "Don't think about it, or it will get you down."

"Yeah, I know. You would think a man would get used to it, not so. It gets harder everytime we move into combat. At first I was so green and scared I didn't have time to worry, now I know. I wonder if this war will ever be over. I'm beginning to think it never will be."

"Oh, it will be over. We might be so old no one will want us."

Their favorite topic, as it was for the rest of the GI's was what they were going to do when they got home.

"The first thing I'm going to do is stand under a hot shower, then eat all of the steak I can hold."

"That's it?"

"No, let me finish. Then I'm going to get my wife into the softest bed I can find, and stay there the rest of my life."

"Now you're bragging."

"I know, but I'm going to give it a try."

The Long Toms had started again, vibrations shook the

ground. It would go on all night—they called it searching fire. Every once in a while tanks would go up to the foot of the mountain, blast for thirty minutes, then make a mad rush out of the combat zone. It would take that long for the Germans to pinpoint their fire. By that time the tankers would be gone.

"Damn tanks, all they're good for is to draw fire. They go in first, get all of the eggs and vino, and then run for it. They never stand and fight."

They had pulled in during Thanksgiving week. He remembered this because everyone had received a fresh orange. Big deal. Now it was almost Christmas and they were still in the same spot. Some of the men were receiving Rest and Relaxation back to Naples. Men drew their names out of a helmet to see who would get to go.

Jacob lined up for evening chow. Luck was with him, and he drew his name. "Well, what do you know, I get to see Naples on the next truck out." He would take a jeep ride back to Corps, then a truck to Seventh Army Headquarters, then another truck to Naples.

Some of the anticipation had worn off by the time they arrived. All of the GIs were dropped off at a staging center, after a short wait their names were called. Again they were in trucks rolling to a rest center. Jacob's truck stopped at what looked to be an old hotel, again their names were called. They were given instructions to catch their trucks back at 5:00 p.m. the day after Christmas.

The sudden jolt into a world of cots with sheets, and plenty of hot water, was almost too much. He put his duffle bag on his cot, stripped down and headed for the showers. It was nice. He stood and let the water run down his head and shoulders. He felt like "Mr. Clean."

All of the GIs were given meal tickets to eat at a nearby cafe. If they had money, they could go wherever they wished. Jacob wanted to get away as far as possible. He didn't pay much attention to the direction he was going, he just took the street that looked the most interesting. He noticed that all of the cars were small. Small motor bikes honked, bells clanged, it was bedlam.

"Joe! Caramella, caramella, caramella, chewing gum."

"Joe, you want a guide?"

48

Glancing up at the sign on the street corner he saw that this was Via Roma. The shop windows didn't have much in them. He wanted to get something to send home.

"Joe, Joe, what you want?"

"I want to buy a scarf."

"A what?"

"Scarf," Jacob made motions around his neck.

"Joe, you pay me, I show you. OK, Joe?"

"OK, how much?"

"One American dollar."

"Fifty cents."

"What's fifty cents? I don't understand."

Jacob held up a fifty cent piece.

"OK Joe, I show you."

The street boy darted ahead, looking back now and then to see if the GI was following. The route led up a side street. It was apparent that it was made up of small, family enterprises with many black market items. Jacob noticed some GI soap and cigarettes for sale.

The street salesman stopped in a stall. Talking very fast, he used his hands to explain; finally he got his desired results. An older woman opened a suitcase full of ties, scarves, and small pieces of jewelry. She carefully laid out all of the scarves, they were nice.

"How much?"

The lady held up five fingers. Through the corner of his eye he could see a small tear rolling down her cheek.

"OK, OK, I'll give her three," he held up three fingers. The lady smiled sadly as she held out the scarf. Jacob was sure there was a story behind the articles in that suitcase. He learned later that people in Naples had turned into small shop keepers as a means of survival. The hard to get items such as soap, cigarettes and candy were goods to barter with.

"OK, Joe."

"OK, thanks."

"Joe, you want a girl? Blond, sixteen and beautiful? I get.

"No, don't bother."

The little salesman was not so easily put off, "You wait." Jacob wasn't interested, but he wondered what the boy would do. He walked in the direction of Via Roma. He wanted to get something to eat then hit the sack for awhile.

"Joe, Joe."

Turning he saw the boy tugging at a young girl. It didn't matter that the girl was larger than he was.

"Joe, Joe, beautiful girl, sixteen."

My God, this girl is just a child. Obviously she was not a streetwalker, nor was she too interested in the confrontation. She hung her head. The boy put his hand under her chin, talking very fast in Italian. She raised her head and managed a weak smile.

"Joe, Joe, you like? Five dollars."

Jesus, these people really must be hungry. It was awful. Jacob reached in his billfold and gave the girl five dollars, "Go home!" She just stood there. He took her by the shoulders and turned her around. "Bona note, good bye." She smiled and started walking; she didn't look back.

Walking toward a sign that said, cafe, he started in.

"Joe, Joe, what's the matter?"

"Nothing. Who was that girl."

"Good girl. My sister."

Jacob suddenly wasn't hungry. He caught a taxi and went back to the rest center.

3

Jacob struggled to regain control. During one period of complete command, he noticed his wife was sitting in a chair asleep. "I don't know what I did to deserve such a woman. I wonder, have I been talking while under the influence of the shots? I hope not. Although I am a preacher, I have not been free from some of the temptations of the world."

In all truth, Jacob had been somewhat of a heller as a young man, not a first class heller, sort of a middle-of-the-road heller. It bothered him, someone might remember the old days.

He had listened to a minister once who had seen a lot of life in frontier towns. "You want some advice son? Whatever you do, don't try to be too good. Whatever it was you did, it's over, forget it. Just charge it to growing up." The old man grinned, "I blame all of my shortcomings on the devil. My wife can tell you that when things come up that I can't explain, my answer is, 'The devil made me.' Her favorite comeback is, 'Old man, don't blame it on the devil, it's just the meanness in all men'."

Again he went under the effects of the shots. It was a hot, muggy night in a small town. It was familiar, yet he couldn't remember its name. Across from where he sat he recognized Yates Furniture Store, a little further down was Holler Cleaners. "That rings a bell, I wonder if Dean Williams still works there? Probably dead, like everyone else in this town."

Getting up and stretching in the same movement, he decided to walk up the street west. On his left a large furniture store

51

loomed, Farmer's Furniture and Undertaking. A postscript read, If you need an undertaker call Am-Pex-6. "That couldn't be right, all telephone numbers have three digits in the prefix. Oh well, it must be the devil."

It was very late, there wasn't a soul on the street. The only noise was the soft, summer breeze blowing through the empty buildings, and the thousands of insects that gathered around the street lights. Crickets were everywhere, he could feel them crunch as he walked on them, they gave a sharp crack, almost like popcorn. As he neared the corner, he thought he saw a man leaning against the lamp post. Hurrying along, he reached the corner. The wind had blown a piece of paper around the post, it was gently waving in the wind. "Jesus, this is weird. I wonder where everyone disappeared, what happened?" Turning right at the next lamp, he crossed the street. Automatically he looked in both directions to see if a car was coming.

Walking north, the street took on a different atmosphere. In the distance he thought he could hear Indian music. "Now I know, this is Indian street. I should know someone here." The only other noise was a faint whisper of the wind. There was nothing, so he took another right. The sign above the store read, Jake Tingley's Pawn Shop. In the store window he saw a few Indian bracelets and some faded shawls. Wow, this was really something.

He felt that he had better get out of here, but it dawned on him that he didn't know where he was. Walking over to the curb, he sat down, "I have to do some thinking." Across the street he noticed a building with a sign, Douglas Drug Store. I've been in that store a lot of times, surely they will be open." Getting up, he walked slowly across the street. Cobwebs covered the entrance, and there was dust on the windows. Medicine bottles laid on the floor. He thought he saw the body of a man on the floor. He tried to open the door, wham! The door fell with a crash, dust flew in all directions. There was a body, or what was left of one. Actually it was more like a skeleton, a few whisps of clothing were around the bones. Apparently small animals had eaten most of his clothes. Backing out, his eyes glued to the remains, he tripped over another body. His reflexes told him to get out, to get out fast. It didn't make sense. He sat down and tried to think. "I know I have been in this town before."

Getting up, he went in the direction of a faint rhythmic sound. There also seemed to be a glow in the sky. "Maybe, just maybe, I can find some life in this town." Running, his lungs straining to inhale more oxygen, he stumbled and fell.

"I think he is coming around. No more shots, let's see how he gets along."

"Jacob."

"Yes."

"You have been so restless, the nurse put up side rails to keep you from falling out of bed. You were hollering, and mumbling words we couldn't understand. You seemed to be crying for help."

"I was lost. I was trying to come back."

"Where were you?"

"I don't know. All I know is that it was a town I used to know very well, yet a place that is no more. Have I been here a long time?"

"Yes, and no. It probably seems like a long time to you, but in terms of days, not long."

"I am all mixed up. I'll be glad when I get out of here."

"I will too."

Ruth was worried. Some of her husband's rambling didn't make sense. The doctor said he was sliding back into his past, it was like a dream. The events in his life that had been pushed aside were now coming to the surface. The next time the doctor made his rounds Ruth quizzed hime about Jocob's restlessness, his mumblings.

"It's nothing unusual. There is no telling what he will say. Whatever it is, don't take it too seriously. The mind and its capacity for memory, is astonishing. He probably will keep it up until he recovers."

"How long will that be?"

"He is getting along very well, a lot faster that I though he could. His vital signs are good."

It was over, the collage of events that he had experienced when in a coma, were over. Jacob felt drained, weak. But, strangely enough, he felt happy. He had not slipped into the

53

darkness for over a day.

When Ruth came into the room, Jacob looked rested. The hospital aid had given him a bath and a fresh gown. He looked good. Ruth couldn't get over the change. Instead of the restlessness she had come to expect, Jacob was ready to talk.

"Ask the old sawbones when I can get out of here."

"Old sawbones?"

"Yes, that's what they called them in the early days. Doctors were not very skilled. When someone's leg or arm was broken, the ride to the doctor's office was often a long one. By then gangrene had usually set in, so the doctor sawed off the broken leg or arm. Antibiotics were unknown. It was like that in the war between the states, no pain killer, no antibiotics. After the war there were a lot of one-legged men. During World War II, very few men lost legs or arms."

"My, you are wound up, you'd better take it easy."

"I've been taking it easy ever since I got here. I'm anxious to eat some home cooking."

"I'll ask the doctor when he makes his rounds."

Almost all hospitals feed early in the evening, the help is always anxious to finish their tour and leave. The sound of dishes and the scent of food filled the hall. Soon a black orderly came in and set Jacob's tray beside him.

"That food smells good, what is it?"

"Some soul food brother. It will get you on the road."

"Tell me about soul food."

"It can be many things. You know all ethnic groups have food that is special to them, something that makes them happy. Among my people it's black-eyed peas, pig's feet, short ribs, all kinds of barbecue with hot sauce." Winking, he added, "And sometimes we have a little ripple to go with it."

"Ripple?"

"That's a special kind of beer that blacks like."

"Sounds good."

"Man, it's the best."

"I might try some of it sometime."

"It would put hair on your chest."

"Not me."

"Why?"

"Indians don't have hair on their chests."

"That's just an expression, it means it would make you stronger. Black men think it makes them horney, I don't know what the women think."

"Come to think of it, maybe I could use some of your food. I certainly need the food, I don't know about the other."

Glancing at Ruth he noticed a faint smile and a blush on her face. "What do you think, Ruth? Should I eat the soul food?"

"That's up to you, I'm ready when you are."

The orderly left with a chuckle; white folks and Indians sure had a lot to learn about lovin'.

"You had better rest, Jacob. You've done a lot of talking, you must be tired."

"You're right, I could use a little Osage exercise."

"I'm going home now, I'll come back this evening." Ruth leaned over and kissed him. "Jacob, you are a rascal, and you a preacher."

"Preachers like to love just like anyone else."

"Yes, I know they do."

As soon as Ruth left the room, Jacob rolled over and was asleep. This time his sleep was peaceful; no wandering, no unknowns.

A few days later Jacob left the hospital. The doctor indicated that he should not exert nor worry. The trip home was joyful; he was alive, life was good, he had much to be thankful for.

Jake was restless. He walked to the window several times looking for his parents' car. He was anxious to see his buddy, they had been in touch with each other. But he felt guilty about wanting to get away. After what seemed like hours he saw their car coming up the drive. Sauntering out to the yard he stood with a wide grin on his face. When the car stopped he opened the door. "I'll help you, Dad."

"I can make it."

"You'd better let me."

"OK."

Jake didn't realize his father was so heavy.

"Over there, I want to sit in that chair on the porch. I just want to look out and see the land and breathe the country air. I'm alright, Jake. I know you have things to do."

"No Dad, I'm not in that much of a hurry. I want to hang around for awhile, the other can wait."

Jacob sat looking out into space, after awhile he relaxed and began to get sleepy. "Jake, I think you need to help me into my room. I'm not as strong as I thought I was."

"OK, Dad." Jake helped him into his bedroom, slipped off his shoes, and covered him with a blanket. His father was asleep almost as soon as he got into the bed.

Jake went outside to his favorite spot, an old rocking chair at the end of the porch. The evening shadows were slowly beginning to show. Everything was at peace; the house was quiet, his mother was napping, his father was sleeping, even he was nodding.

But Jacob's dreaming wasn't over. This time he was in his own backyard, sitting under a tree talking to Jake. "Son, you have a puzzled look on your face."

"Well, I've been thinking I need a car of my own, so I went looking today."

"How did it go?"

"I don't understand the buying of a car. I went down to the Ford dealer's—it was a strange experience."

"What was so strange about it?"

"I started looking at some of the cars on the lot, and a salesman with a big smile on his face came out. He shoved his hand at me and gave me his name. Then I asked him how much for the car I liked. He wouldn't tell me, he wanted to know if I had a trade-in. I explained that I didn't. Then he said, 'Son, let's go to my office,' so we walked into a little cubbyhole. 'If you want to pay cash for that car, we can let you have it for say, eleven thousand, plus dealer's prep., plus dealer's freight cost. Let's see: air, trim, power, we will throw in. Oh yes, there is a small charge for the racing stripes.' He took out a calculator and began totaling all of the extra costs. It was something like fourteen thousand for a cash deal."

"He wanted to know if I had a credit rating, so I said, 'What's that?' He said, 'I don't know, boy. Your credit don't sound too good to me. Can you pay cash?'

"About that time I walked out, with the salesman on my heels.

I told him to get lost, but he started after me again. I told him, 'I don't want to hear any more out of you, not one word, or I'll deck you.' That was about it. It made me mad.''

"Jake, that's one of life's jolts. I, too, hate to buy a car, I hate to go through the hassle. It's what I call the 'salesman's fertility rite,' especially a car salesman. I saw this advertisement last night on the television, where the owner was saying how happy they would be to sell a car. Son, you never meet the owner. I don't know where they stay, certainly not among the customers. Don't let it get you down. When I get on my feet I'll go with you. I know how to handle those wise guys.''

"Jacob, do you feel like coming to the table? It's time to eat.''
"Let me wash my face, it seems like all I do is sleep.''
Jake poked his head in the door, "Need any help, Dad?''
"No, I need to use my legs. Lying around in the hospital made me weak.''

Ruth and Jake watched Jacob as he walked slowly to the table. He made it without any difficulty. Automatically they bowed their heads, "We thank you, oh Lord, for the gift of life, for family and friends. We are blessed to have the opportunity to serve you. Bless the leaders of the world, grant them wisdom. In all our efforts, help us to direct our lives toward helping others. Grant us physical strength, Amen.'' The atmosphere radiated happiness, it was as if a great weight had been lifted off their shoulders.''

"It's good to have my feet under this table again.''
"It's good to have you, Dad.''

Ruth didn't say anything. Her face radiated the story, it was very obvious. They were all at peace. Their evening meal over, they excused themselves. Jake went to the porch to watch for Robert, Ruth went to the kitchen, and Jacob felt he needed to rest for a few minutes.

Jacob dreamed of an old classmate, a Cheyenne who had recently died. It was like a mini-movie.

John Blackfoot was seventy-nine years of age when he was hospitalized because of a minor stroke. During the night he had a heart attack and died. The word went out like a bolt of lightning. John was a prominent Indian, a chief, a member of the Black Leggins Society. He attended all the powwows in the area of Clinton, Canton and Colony.

He was a quiet man who seldom raised his voice in protest. He gave his counsel and sat down. If someone wanted to argue, it would have to be with someone else. In this fashion, he made few enemies and many friends. The Brown Funeral Home handled all of the Indian funerals. How it started no one knew, but it had long since been the custom. After the body was prepared for burial, his family came and took it home.

John's house was small, but it was not a rental house. He and his wife were proud of the fact that the house was theirs, they had paid for it out of John's wages.

Also, as was the custom, people brought in food; some cooked, some that needed cooking.

From the time the casket was placed in the house, a continuous flow of people came by. Some stopped long enough to say a prayer, some helped in the kitchen, serving coffee and food to the visitors. Some of the men took their places at the drum, others relieved tired singers. This went on all night.

A few of John's white friends dropped by in the early evening. They sat for awhile all eyes and ears. One of them whispered, "They all sound alike." Another said, "If you have heard one Indian song, you have heard all of them." Little did they know that this was about as far from the truth as possible. There are different songs, different tempos and rhythms. The tempo of Cheyenne music is nothing like Pueblo or Navajo music.

The night drug on, by now most of the mouners had paid their respects and left for home. Only members of the gourd clan and a few women in the kitchen remained.

John's wife gave in at 2:00 a.m. Her daughters put her to bed, one of them sat with her. The women in the kitchen knew what to do. They started cooking breakfast. One lady washed the dishes from the night-sing, another cleaned off the kitchen table. Soon they announced, "Breakfast is ready." It didn't take any urging. All of the men were tired, they were also hungry.

By the time all of the men had eaten, the funeral director, along with his helpers, came for the body. They had worked Indian funerals before, they were efficient, caring professionals.

They had long ago learned the ritual of Cheyenne and Arapaho funerals; they knew that a member of the gourd clan would go with the body and stay with it until the grave was closed.

John's funeral was attended by throngs of people. They could not all get into the church. The funeral was scheduled for two o'clock. That really didn't mean anything. It would start on Indian time, that being when all of the preachers arrived and everything was ready.

Jacob rolled over and blinked his eyes. For a moment he didn't know where he was. Then he looked out of the window. He was at home.

Robert Gombi wheeled into his yard in Lawton. Since school was out he had been doing his best to burn the candle at both ends. Summertime was the good time, it was the time for living and loving. His father was standing on the porch as Robert drove up, he had a frown on his face. He knew young bucks wanted it all, in a hurry.

"Son, I need to talk to you."

"OK, Dad."

"Indian elders feel that it is their obligation to teach their children the way of their tribes. We are proud of you, still we don't want you to get hurt, or to bring sorrow on your tribe."

"What do you mean, Dad?"

"Let me explain. I know you have been restricted by living at Riverside School. Now you want to kick up your heels. We want you to have a good time, but not at the expense of others."

"Like what?"

"All the parents of the girls you have been dating are also proud of their daughters, they don't want any shame to come to them."

"But Dad, they are so willing. They like my lovin', I guess they like me."

"Now you're bragging, boy. I understand your liking them. I understand that they might be willing to make love with you, however, I must insist that you be very careful. I don't want any mother coming over here and telling me that my son has to marry her daughter. It would cause a lot of unhappiness to everyone. If you have to go after a girl, be sure she is someone you can be

59

proud of. You might want to marry her."

"No, Dad. I don't want to marry. I have many things that I need to do before that. OK, I'll be careful.

"Oh, by the way, I'm going to visit Jake and his family. I might stay two or three days. Anything else?"

"That's about it. Keep that monster you drive under control, the State Highway Patrol is on the prowl for guys like you."

"Dad, can I use the pickup? I promise not to be gone over three days. If something comes up, you can always reach me at Jake's."

"OK, you know where I keep the keys. How are you fixed for money?"

"I'm just about broke."

"I figured you would be. Here's three tens."

"Thanks. I really need to see Jake."

"Keep away from fast girls."

"OK."

It wasn't all that far to Jake's, he had covered the road many times. One thing he really wanted to know was what happened with Mary Marie. Girls were always soft for him. "I bet a dead dog that he really made time with her. If he didn't, I sure am. That girl sure did sound like something special."

Riding along with the window open, Robert kept the beat of the music on the steering wheel. Thoughts danced through his head. "I've got to find someone to love, this hop, skip, and jump style won't get it.

"Man, I've got to be careful, I can't go to sleep. I've got too many things to do." Mile after mile, the rhythm of the slapping of the tires sang its own song. Occasionally an insect would be pulled inside by the suction of the wind. Once a bee came in, causing him to pull over to the bar ditch. As he did, the bee left on its own. He fought drowsiness, bugs, heat and thirst until he reached Jake's.

Summertime at Hog Creek Mission was sleepy time, the sun beat down with a vengence. Everyone in this area enjoyed living under an arbor, the out-of-doors residence of many Plains Indians. It served as a place for cooking, eating, or sleeping or beading. Since it didn't have any walls, what breeze there was could flow through.

The two boys were glad to see each other. Having spent so

much time together at school, they had much in common. Today, Robert was the aggressor, he wanted some information. "Old buddy, how did you make out with Mary Marie?"

Jake was stoic, "Oh, nothing much went on. I went over to her home, spent about a week. We talked and went swimming, that's about all."

"Come on, surely more happened than you've filled me in on. How about the loving, and such?"

"Well, there was a little loving, but not much 'and such'."

"Man, you are sure closed mouthed. Surely something must have happened."

"A gentleman doesn't tell everything."

"A gentlman, my ass, you're a long way from a gentleman."

Jake refused to get mad, he was holding the high cards.

"Now that's not any way to treat your old buddy. Remember me. I'm Robert."

"Well, why don't you ask her?"

"That's what I'm going to do."

"When?"

"In a few days."

Now it was Jake's turn to ask a few questions. "Tell me, how you doing with the girls?"

"Oh, I've been seeing a few here and there, nothing serious. My dad sorta laid down the hard line on me, said he didn't want any girl's mother coming over to talk about marriage."

"Hey, you must have been making some time with those Kiowa girls."

"A little."

"Why are you barking up Mary Marie's tree?"

"I think you know. Those Kiowa girls are too easy, besides, you made that girl sound terrific."

"You want something special?"

"Yes."

"Take a tip from your old buddy, she's special. But I doubt if she will be receptive."

"Why do you say that, did you put your brand on her?"

"No, I didn't. I don't think any man will be able to lead her to the altar. She really doesn't need a man, she has all of the money she needs, and then some. She's related to the Mellons of Pittsburgh, Pennsylvania."

"Never heard of them."

"They have earned a good share of the money in Pittsburgh."

"Oh. And she likes you?"

"I'm not sure. But son, she can have any man she wants."

"Don't 'son' me, I think you're lying."

"As I said before, why don't you give it a try?"

"You're too confident, something is not right."

"The best way to find out is for yourself."

Robert's hackles were raised, he was mad. He knew he had to get out of there, now. "I'll be seein' ya." He took off in his pickup, not sure of where he was going. "Damn the luck, I didn't think old Jake had it in him to act this way with his old buddy."

He was in this frame of mind as the afternoon passed. Before he realized it, he was coming to the outskirts of Oklahoma City. He noticed that his gas tank was getting low. The first service station was a nondescript building with flashing red lights advertising Coors beer. "It sure doesn't look like a service station to me, but as long as they sell gas I guess it will do." He didn't see any self-service pumps. After waiting for a few minutes, he went into the building. There was a girl behind the cash register. "How about gettin' some gas?"

"Some gas? Boy, those pumps haven't had gas in them for over five years."

"What do you have them out there for?"

"They are left over from the old days."

"What do you sell?"

"Girls."

"You mean this is a cat house?"

"You called it boy, any girl in the house for five dollars."

"I never paid for any in my life."

"Ours are the best kind."

"Oh yeah?"

"You wouldn't know, you don't look like you're dry behind the ears."

"I'm old enough to know I'm not going to buy one of your girls."

This made the girl mad, and she yelled, "Carlos, there's a rube out here looking for trouble."

That was enough, Robert hit the steps flying. He was in his pickup and down the road before any trouble could start. "Damned whorehouse. Man, I tell you this, I'm going to be careful where I stop the next time." Robert drove past several stations when he saw a big Texaco sign. It proved to be what he was looking for. It had everything: help yourself gas, free road maps, along with road information.

He had decided his next stop would be Hominy, Oklahoma and Mary Marie. Then an awful thought popped into his mind, "What if she isn't home, or what if she won't see me? But I'm not going to let old Jake get ahead of me. I've got to find out."

Robert had studied his Oklahoma map and had turned off of I-35 at Perry. But he failed to notice he had to turn north at Cleveland. Before he knew it, he was in Westport, a jerkwater town consisting of one service station and a chili parlor. Wheeling around, he pulled into the station. An old rooster was vigorously scratching in the drive. The screen door was ajar, so he walked in and saw a body on a makeshift couch. "Jesus, this guy could be dead." Suddenly a loud snore broke the stillness. "He's not dead...could be drunk...but I don't think so."

Robert realized he couldn't get any information here. "Maybe the crowd at the chili joint will know." The jukebox was blaring **Yellow Rose of Texas.** The place was jumping. Men, women and children were crammed in a place no larger that a good sized box. Robert went over to a man who didn't seem to be too interested in anything except eating chili. "Say, mister, where is the road to Hominy?"

No answer.

"Hum, must be hard of hearing." Speaking in a much louder voice Robert said, "Where is the road to Hominy?"

Slowly, slowly the man turned around. "Boy, let me tell you something. I'm not deaf."

"Well, you didn't answer my question."

"Didn't feel like answering it."

Robert felt like he was in the wrong place. The man kept on eating, he didn't miss a beat, slurp, slurp to the tune of the music. When he finished, he turned around. "Boy, where did you say you wanted to go?"

"Hominy."

"No use to go there."

"Why?"

"That town's dead, been dying a long time."

"Could be, but I don't think the girl I'm looking for is dead."

"What's her name?"

"Mary Marie Tinker."

"You looking for that Osage girl?"

"Yes."

"Save your time and money."

"What do you mean?"

"That gal doesn't have anything to do with the folks around here. I've heard she is wild, man, wild."

"Could be, but I'd like to find out for myself."

"OK by me."

"Now which is the road to her house?"

The man got off of his stool and walked out the door past the gasoline pumps. He stopped in the middle of the road and pointed toward the west. "Up that road yonder, until you come to a fork in the road, then go north. Son, that will put you smack-dab on the road to Hominy. Still, I would advise you against going. You don't look like no tenderfoot, still I hate to see a young man taken in."

"I'll take my chances."

"It's your funeral."

"Thanks for your help."

The old man went off mumbling to himself, "Dern fool kids, can't tell them nothing. That girl will eat him up like a toad frog. I've been talking to so many dern, fool crazies, they have me talking to myself."

At Cleveland, Robert pulled in at the same service station that Jake had stopped at some weeks before. Also, the same two men were arguing about the Democrats and the Republicans. They didn't pay any attention to him so he walked over to them and said, "I need some information."

No response.

"This is a strange country, no ne wants to talk." Somewhat louder, he said, "I need some information."

No response.

He noticed a Coke box nearby so he dropped a quarter in, but nothing came out. Robert was getting irritated. "What's the matter with this machine, I didn't get any Coke out of it."

One of the men slowly turned, "No wonder, it's broken."

"How about getting my money back."

"Can't do that."

"Why?"

"I can't get in the box. The Coke man has the key."

"You can get it out of your cash register."

"Can't do that. Don't have one."

"Where do you keep your money?"

"Can't tell you."

"Why not?"

"You might be a robber."

"Do I look like a robber, or a gunman?"

"Could be, you never can tell."

"Forget it, old man."

"Who's old?"

"Just a figure of speech."

"A what?"

"Nothing, forget it. Can you tell me where a girl by the name of Mary Marie Tinker lives?"

"Yes, I know where she lives, saw her go by here just yesterday. Dern fool Osage, gonna kill herself driving like mad."

"I just want to know where she lives."

"Your bad luck."

"Why do you say that?"

"Because she's a wild, wild woman. Want some advise?"

"No. Well, just a little."

"Boy, she will swallow you up like a tornado."

"Bad, huh?"

"Some guy is always looking for her. If I was a young buck I might do the same." He took off his hat and scratched his head. "That girl has everything; looks, money, but she's wild."

"I like them wild."

"Hope so." Walking out into the road he pointed to the north and said, "Get on that road and go about eight miles. You'll see it, she lives in a mansion by herself, with only one black servant. I don't know what goes on; some say wild parties, drinking, naked men and women."

"Have you ever been there?"

"Who me? Not on your life, my wife would kill me." Chuckling, he added, "Might go, if no one would find out."

"Thanks, old man, I'll be seeing you." All Robert could hear was some mumbling.

After some time spent on the road, Robert became aware of

a large house in the distance. That must be it. The old man said it was a mansion, so he expected it to be fairly large, but as he approached the house it appeared even larger. Driving up the circular drive, he could feel some of his bravado leaving. He couldn't get over it. As the man said, the house was a mansion.

He pushed the bell, "What the hell, I've got nothing to lose." He waited and waited.

The door was opened by a black servant. "Yes?"

"I'm Robert, would you tell Mary Marie that I'm here?"

The servant looked at him carefully, "I'm sorry, but were you here before?"

"No."

"Hum, you sure look like someone that was here not long ago. If you will go around to the back, there is a swimming pool and cabana. Miss Tinker is out there. You can't miss it, just follow the gravel path."

"Thanks."

"Yes, sir."

Robert followed the instructions. Rounding the line of clipped hedges, he could hear music. From behind a chaise lounge he could see two feet sticking out. Clearing his throat so that he wouldn't startle Mary Marie, he came up to her. "I'm sorry, I didn't mean to frighten you. I'm Robert Gombi from Lawton."

"Are you part of the dream?"

He didn't understand exactly what she meant, but he said, "Yes."

She looked at him through half closed lids, "Go over to the bar and pour yourself a drink. There are some sandwiches in the pool refrigerator, that is, if you're hungry."

Robert was in a state of shock. "Jesus, she is beautiful." He got himself a small drink and a sandwich.

"Come over and sit down. I don't have much company, but then, the townspeople don't approve of me."

"So?" Robert was looking at the house. In his wildest dreams he didn't think Mary Marie would live in a house like this.

"What's the matter? You don't seem very talkative?"

"I guess I wasn't ready for a place like this." Grasping for words he said, "Jake told me he was here."

"Yes, he was here for three or four days, then he had to go home because his father had a heart attack."

"Do you like Jake?"

"Yes, I enjoyed seeing him."

"Are you going to marry him?"

"He never asked me."

"Would you?"

"I don't know. Sure I like him, but marriage is a different thing. I would have to be very sure about anyone I marry." Mary Marie looked closely at Robert, "What's the matter, are you sick?"

"No, I guess all of this is just so sudden. I really didn't expect anything like this."

"Have another drink, you'll feel better soon. I'm sure the long drive in this heat has been too much for you."

He filled his glass with soda, then poured a little bourbon in it. Getting up his nerve he managed a better look at Mary Marie. "That's not much of a swimsuit."

"It's called a string bikini. Haven't you seen a naked girl, Robert?"

"No ma'am."

"No ma'am? Do I look that old?"

Now he was confused. "No, you don't look old. You are beautiful!"

"Thank you. When you finish your drink, we could go for a swim."

"I don't have a suit."

"That's alright, I never wear a suit when I swim. Don't worry, there's no one around, this is a very private place."

The food and drink had helped, his nerves quit screaming. He had not been used to hard liquor, so he could feel the jolt. As a matter of fact, he began to feel brave, almost too brave.

"I really came up here to see you, not to talk about Jake."

"That's nice. I think you two boys are real nice young men."

"Well, I don't know about the last part."

"You mean you are somewhat of a playboy?"

"Not exactly. To tell the truth, I have never had a girl."

"Had a girl? You mean you have never had intercourse with a girl?"

"No, I haven't. I'm somewhat of a greenhorn around girls."

"I think you have the right idea."

"I just don't know how to go about it. I'm sure girls think I'm something of a country boy."

"I think you are nice. Don't let the fact that you haven't been around bother you. Guys these days expect every girl to fall for them. I call them bed hoppers."

"Bed hoppers? I don't understand."

"The only thing they are interested in is getting a girl into bed. No love, no caring, no tenderness, just plain, raw sex. I'll tell you something, Robert, I don't like that. I'd rather know a man like you, one that a girl could trust and love, not one of those bed hoppers."

"I understand. Take my word for it, I'm not a bed hopper."

"I'm sorry, Robert, I didn't mean to unload on you."

"That's alright, now I know what kind of men you like."

"Let's go for a swim, Robert, we've had enough talking." Walking to the pool, she took off her halter and string bikini, and dived in with a single motion.

"God, that girl is beautiful, I think she's wonderful. Oh, man!" Robert just stood, watching her.

"Aren't you coming?"

"I'll be right there." Turning his back to Mary Marie, he removed his clothing as speedily as possible, and dived into the pool like a river rat.

"What took you so long? You're not afraid of me are you?"

"No." He wanted to say, yes, but he had to sound brave.

Mary Marie swam up to him, put both of her arms around his neck, and gave him a very wet kiss. The closeness of her body had him steaming, he was embarrassed. Realizing that she had him very worked up, she swam to the other end of the pool and got out. "Come on out."

"Be right with you." He went down to the end of the pool, by the time he got to his clothes he was dry. Looking around, he didn't see Mary Marie, she had disappeared, but probably not for long. He decided the thing to do was wait. He poured himself another small drink, and was eating a sandwich when she returned. She had slipped into a sun dress with matching shoes.

"You know you are the most beautiful girl I have every known, just looking at you makes my day complete."

"Thanks. Let me tell you, I'm no angel."

"I think you are."

"I've been up to the house. My servant is a good cook, loves to entertain. I think you will enjoy his cooking. Do you want to stay over? There are alot of rooms in this house."

"Yes, if your room is close to mine."

"Right next door, so if you get scared I'll come to your rescue."

"That's not what I was thinking about."

"What were you thinking?"

"That we sleep in the same room."

Mary Marie looked at Robert a long time. Slowly she said, "I'll tell you, Robert, I don't go sleeping around. If you want a one-night stand there are girls in Hominy that will give you your money's worth."

"I'm sorry, Mary Marie, I didn't mean to make you mad. I was just thinking."

"I know what you were thinking, and I don't blame you for trying. Just like I said, I have to be in the mood, and really go for the guy before I get in bed with him. Come on, let's eat."

The servant had prepared cold, sliced turkey, creamed asparagus, and new potatoes and peas. On the side there was a glass of sparkling wine.

Robert seated Mary Marie. She accepted the courtesy with a smile. The food was excellent. Soon the servant offered a platter for him to take some more. He was hungry, he did justice to the meal. "That was good."

"Thanks, my servant loves to cook. What is left of the meal he takes home to his family, so he always cooks more than will be eaten. Robert, would you like to take a ride, we have some good riding stock."

"Hey, that would be nice."

"Will you excuse me for awhile, I need to see my servant."

"Sure, call me when you're ready." Robert wondered if her servant had a name. She kept calling him, my servant, somehow it didn't wear.

Mary Marie's servant did, indeed, have a very unusual name, Gustavo. He had come from Cuba with a great many others when Castro opened the gates. He had worked in a Grand Hotel in Cuba, so he knew the high and mighty who came to gamble and womanize. Generally life had been good to him, but there were no opportunities left in Cuba. He had the American dream, to be a businessman, to make it big.

Mary Marie's father knew him in the gala days of Cuba. He

69

had urged Gustavo to come to Oklahoma. So when he left Cuba, his mind was on one thing—to find Senor Tinker. Upon arrival his family was tired and hungry. They made a call, and arrangements were made for them to come to the big house in Hominy.

Mary Marie's father had not lived long after they arrived. It did not matter, Gustavo had said to himself, "I will stay as long as his daughter is single, when she marries I will go into business for myself." He was devoted to Mary Marie; a protector, a friend, in a way, a father.

"Gustavo, will you go to town and get Rosa? I have a young buck who has never had a woman, I think Rosa will fill the bill. Here, give her this," she handed Gustavo a fifty dollar bill.

"I don't think she will take this much."

"I want her to give her best."

"What time do you want her?"

"Any time after ten will do."

"Yes, Miss Tinker."

"I'm a devil, I know, but I think Robert will enjoy her."

After their ride they were hungry again. As they went upstairs to their rooms, Mary Marie said, "I thought we would eat in a small room off my dad's library, it's a favorite spot of mine. Come down when you're dressed."

"It won't take long."

"No hurry."

Mary Marie didn't take the small elevator down, she deliberately walked, very slowly, down the massive staircase, taking time to admire some of her father's pictures on the wall. There were memories...mostly good...some sad.

She passed through her father's library to the small adjacent room. It was a pleasant, comfortable place with a serving table, buffet, and a built-in refrigerator. Gustavo had prepared a snack before leaving. She fussed with the flowers, adjusted the silverware, and inspected the napkins. Mary Marie was happy, she enjoyed having guests.

"Here you are, did you have any trouble finding this room?"

"No, I just followed your perfume."

"Do you like it?"

"Very much, it's nice."

"Sit here where you can get a good view. This is one of my favorite rooms in the house, it brings back many happy moments with my dad." Mary Marie served the food. "Will you pour the champagne? I'm sure it's chilled."

"I never did serve champagne."

"Take that corkscrew by the ice bucket, screw it in the cork, then pull. It will probably make a loud pop, champagne always has a lot of body.

Robert followed the instructions, even to the loud pop, and managed to pour the champagne into the chilled glasses. The food was excellent, and the champagne began to loosen him up. He felt talkative, generous, warm; his emotions completely engulfed him.

Mary Marie looked at him out of the corner of her eye. "I have a surprise for you."

"Good or bad?"

"Very good."

"Tell me, Mary Marie," Robert coaxed.

"No, it's a surprise, you will have to be patient."

"This all seems like a dream, I hope I'll never wake up."

"This may appear to be never-never land, but believe me it's real. When you start out on your way home, reality will set in."

Back and forth, the evening was filled with talk of days gone by and days to come. Robert found himself talking about his years at Riverside Indian School. Mary Marie was a good listener, when he slowed down she managed to insert a question.

"Hey, I've been doing all of the talking, what about you?"

"Well, the first years of my life were the good years. Both my mother and father were living, they loved each other very much. I traveled with my mother when she made her trips back east. My parents also made a trip to Europe once a year. They filled the house with art treasures. There were years of sadness, too. I don't really want to talk about it, but briefly, my mother tried to entertain in this big house, it didn't work out." Mary Marie sat for a long time without saying a word. Robert could see it was painful for her.

"I'm sorry, I didn't mean to cause you any unhappiness."

"It's over, the pain is still there, but I can handle it. Come on let's take a walk." The night was beautiful, the gravel path reflected the moonlight. It helped Mary Marie, she was again her

71

cheerful self. "I know, let's go for a swim."

"Don't you think we should wait for our meal to settle?"

"It's been more than forty-five minutes, and I'm ready." Mary Marie walked over to a beach chair. Using it for a clotheshorse, she was undressed and in the pool before Robert could get started. "Come on in! Are you always so slow?"

"No, I'll be there in a minute." Robert was still in awe of Mary Marie. So far his trip had been very, very interesting, and he wondered how the rest of the evening would turn out.

He thought he was a good swimmer, but he couldn't keep up with Mary Marie, she was just too good. Back and forth she swam. When she came to the end of the pool she would flip over and kick off under water. She covered the length of the pool without effort. Robert was a river swimmer, he didn't know the fancy strokes. His efforts were rather crude, compared to hers. "Hey, you are a good swimmer."

"Thanks, it's just part of my life." Mary Marie climbed out and wrapped herself in a large beach towel. Robert managed to do the same. He definitely felt put down by Mary Marie's swimming exhibition.

"Come on, old chap, don't take it so hard. If you had been swimming as much as I have, you'd be an excellent swimmer. How about a drink before turning in? Pour yourself a bourbon, and one for me."

"OK." The drink helped , he lost some of his poor-me feeling.

"If you are hungry, remember there is food in the pool refrigerator."

"Thanks, but I'll just stick with my drink."

"Sleepy?"

"Yes, a little, swimming always relaxes me."

"Don't forget about the surprise."

"Oh, I haven't forgotten. Any clues?"

"Sorry, it wouldn't be a surprise. Let's stay here for awhile. I just want to look at the millions of stars in the heavens." They relaxed in their beach chairs; not a human sound, only the sounds of the night, crickets and locusts. A long distance down the road a bullfrog sounded off to let everyone know of his territorial rights. This wasn't exactly heaven, but for Robert it was very close. He wished it could go on forever. Without realizing it he dozed off. The next thing he knew, Mary Marie was shaking him. "Are you ready to turn in for the night?"

Robert was not fully awake, "Yes, yes I'm ready."

"This way remember?"

He didn't remember, but he said, "Yeah, I remember."

"Don't forget about the surprise."

This remark really woke him up, his mind cleared as if hit by a cold shower. "You mean...?"

"Yes, this very night."

"Oh, my God," Robert thought, "what have I gotten myself into? I'm not ready, I've never had a girl before. I don't want to get married, what if she gets pregnant."

"Come on, what's the matter? Don't you want to?"

"Yes, I want you."

Mary Marie could not keep the smile off of her face. "Here we are. Now the first thing you do is go into the bath and take a shower, you have to be sweet and clean."

"Oh, my God," he thought, "she really means it." He said, "OK, I'll take my shower, you go get ready."

"Don't be too long."

"I won't."

As soon as Mary Marie was out of the room, Robert got his bag out of the closet, picked up his extra shirt, and was gone. He went down the flight of stairs like the devil was after him. Jumping into his pickup, he headed down the road for Cleveland. his mind was functioning on all cylinders. "Boy, that was close. I almost made an ass out of myself."

Mary Marie heard the front door slam. She went downstairs and opened the front door, all she could see was a cloud of dust. Well I'll be damned, I wouldn't have believed it. Our ardent lover was all bark and no bite. Then she saw a small compact car turn into the drive, it was Rosa.

"Senorita, I'm sorry I am a little late."

"It doesn't matter, that cloud of dust was made by your date for tonight."

"I don't understand."

"Come on in, let's have some coffee and I'll explain." Over coffee and scones, Mary Marie explained everything and they both had a good laugh.

"So the big lover turned out to be a pussycat. Well, you know how some men are."

73

"Yes, I know. I think he was still a boy with big ideas."

"I hope it doesn't scare him for the rest of his life."

"It probably won't. You'll get the money just the same, but I'm sorry it didn't turn out better. Why don't you spend the night since you're here? I love having company, and we have lots of room."

"Alright, I would like that. I could sleep in one of the big beds and dream I was back in Cuba."

"Dream anything you like, it's on the house. Why don't you use this room? It was Robert's, but as you know, he won't be using it tonight." They both laughed. "When you put your things away, come into my room, and we'll talk some more. I'm glad, in a way, that the evening turned out like it did."

"Yes, but it's hard on my ego."

"Don't worry, there will another day."

"That's right. I'll be in shortly."

Robert was so upset that he drove nonstop to his home. Everyone was asleep except his mother. She knocked gently on his door, "Have a good time son?"

"The best."

"That's good. Good night."

"Good night, wake me about seven. I want to talk to Jake."

"Alright, see you in the morning."

Robert was beat, the last few hours had been a real drag. When he hit the sack the hours passed like minutes. In the middle of the afternoon he was awakened by the sound of a honking horn and a loud voice. He would know that voice anywhere, it was Jake. There was a loud knock on his door. "Hey, lover boy! It's time to rise and shine."

"OK, OK."

"Well, how was your trip, and did you see Mary Marie?"

"Good...and yes."

"Tell me about it. No lies, boy, I want it straight from the horse's mouth. You look terrible, so you must have had a good time."

"First of all I need a shower, then something to eat, with some black, black coffee."

"OK, I'll go shoot the breeze with your mother."

74

Robert was groggy, it was hard for him to get started. After a shower, he began to think he was alive. Now, for something to eat and some Indian coffee.

"Here you are son, your breakfast is ready, just the way you like it."

Jake had turned a chair around, putting his arms on the back. "Man, you have it made. With a setup like this you probably never will leave home. Even Mary Marie couldn't get you away from this." Jake was trying his best to find out what went on at Mary Marie's, but he didn't find out anything as Robert wasn't talking.

"I understand, old boy, you don't want to talk about your trip. But you can tell your old pal, Jake, anything. It will stop at that point."

"Oh, yeah? It would be like putting it in the **Anadarko Daily News!**"

"No, on my honor, I won't tell a thing. You know gentlemen never talk."

Silence.

"OK, if that's the way you want it."

"That's the way I want it."

"Say, I have some big news," Jake said. "You want to hear it?"

"Sure, if it's really news."

Jake put on his sober face, "Well, my dad has accepted a church in Kansas."

"Where?"

"Big Bend, Kansas."

"Never heard of it."

"Me neither, really it isn't a town, just a rural post office. I looked on the map, but it's not on the map."

"Tell me more."

"Well, from Tulsa you go north to Independence, Kansas. Big Bend is someplace between Independence and Chanute."

"Sounds exciting."

"It is to my dad and mother. You know my mother is from that part of Kansas, she says all of the people are big wheat and cattle farmers. My dad's church is rural one, and there's a house that goes with it. I'm glad for my dad, he wants to make a change. All of us are happy."

"Any girls up there."

75

"I don't know, bound to be though. Most of the ranch people have large families."

"Well, there is nothing like a good old-fashioned country girl. I've heard they like lovin'."

"You know, I'm going to miss this place, especially your homely face."

"Well, look who's talking, Mr. America, God's gift to women."

There was a noticeable lull in the conversation. Deep down they knew this was probably the end of an era. Certainly they would not be seeing each other as much as before. They were sad, but neither wanted to show it. They tied on a face of self-confidence, with a lot of macho.

Jake had an idea. "Well, good buddy, let's do something. We could go for a swim in Randlett Park in Anadarko. We might meet some babes."

"OK by me."

When they got there both of the boys put on a good show, but their hearts were not in it. The water was fine. The babes were there, as a matter of fact they were almost run over by girls who were eager for attention.

"See anything you like?" asked Jake.

"Nope, not a thing. They look very young to me, San Quentin quail! Yeah, looks like jail bait to me."

Finally both boys found a girl they considered acceptable. "Hey, girls, you get dressed. We will meet you in my pickup, it's the dark blue one with wire wheels."

"OK, we'll be out in a few minutes."

Jake knew all of the quiet spots. His favorite was under a bridge not far from the pool. "You girls want a beer?" They didn't look old enough, but what the heck.

"Yes, make it Coors."

Jake drove over to the nearest convenience store, bought a six-pack and headed for the bridge. Arriving at this favorite spot, they unloaded, split the beer, and went in different directions.

Spreading out a groundsheet, Jake lay in the shade and popped a beer. He hadn't really looked at his pick up, now he could see that she might be sixteen, maybe seventeen. "Say, how old are you? Also, what's your name?"

"Hey, you're full of questions."

"I'm sorry, I just don't like to take out any jail bait."

"Well, for your information, my name is Sheri, and I'm sixteen. Don't worrry, I know all about the facts of life. My mother gives me contraceptives, she doesn't want me getting pregnant."

"Nice mother."

"Well, big boy, do you want to make love, or do you want to sit around and ask questions? Let's split another beer, I think you need it."

"Probably do."

After their third beer, Sheri started to undress, "Now I think I'm in the mood, I hope you are."

Actually she was very attractive; nice body, young, and willing.

"Hey, get your clothes off, I don't like to make love to a man with his clothes on."

"Damn."

"What's the matter? You did bring me out here to make love didn't you? I have my clothes off, but you are standing there like a stuffed turkey."

"I'll show you who's a turkey! Come over here, I need help. My zipper is caught and I can't get my britches off."

"You know what I think?"

"I'm not interested in what you think."

"I don't think you ever had a woman."

"Look who's talkin', you're a long ways from being a woman. I think you two are just a couple of punk girls."

"Who's a punk."

"You are."

"You say one more word and I'm leaving."

"Looking like that."

"Oh, my God, I forgot, I don't have any clothes on." But Sheri couldn't leave well enough alone; "What I wanted was a man, instead I came up with a greenhorn boy."

Jake was boiling. He reached over to Sheri, grabbed her wrist, and pulled her over his knee. He then proceeded to give her a spanking. Sheri let out a cry like a wounded goose.

Robert and his girl, hearing the scream, came running. "What's going on?"

"Nothing, nothing at all."

"Sounded like someone was getting killed."

Jake had dropped Sheri to the ground. She lay there whimpering, not loud, somewhere between a cry and a laugh. She looked at Jake, "I'm sorry, I didn't mean to call you a turkey, but you made me mad."

"You made me mad, too."

Sheri walked over to Jake and threw her arms around him, sand, tears and all. Nuzzling up to Jake, she took a big bite on his ear. With a cry, he pushed her away. Sheri snatched up her clothes and took off up the river.

"Let her go, Jake. Let's get out of here."

Robert's girl was stunned, "You can't leave me here."

"That's exactly what we are going to do."

"What about Sheri?"

"What about her?" Robert grumbled. "If she ever stops running she can walk home."

The boys managed to get their clothes on. "With our luck the truck won't start," but it did. Roaring down the lane, they didn't stop until they hit the main road.

"Think we'll get into trouble dumping those girls at the river?"

"Nope."

"You sound very sure."

"Yep. I recognized your girl, she's been sleeping around with half the guys in Anadarko."

"You mean she's a hooker?"

"No, she's not a hooker, she just likes to sleep around. Forget it.!"

"God, if my folks knew what I've been doing they would be very, very unhappy. I guess I've got a lot to learn, I don't think it's right to treat people that way."

"You're probably right, but you know as well as I do that those two girls are nothing but tramps."

"What does that make us?"

"Will you quit it? I said everything will be alright."

"I hope so."

The rest of the trip home nothing was said, the fun was over. A cloud had moved in, lighthing had struck, a new dimension had entered their lives, a new wrinkle showed on their faces. All of the bravado, all of the devil-may-care attitude was gone. They were growing up, their boyhood had been left behind. For this they were sad.

They drove into Jake's yard. Robert put his things in his pickup and drove off calling, "I'll be seein' ya."

Jake's mother was waiting on the porch. "Did you and Robert have a falling out?"

"No, Mother, we just did a little growing up today."

"Want to talk about it?"

"No...not today. Maybe sometime...but not today."

"Jake, we have a lot to do; packing, getting ready to leave. I'm glad you're here."

"When do we have to be in Big Bend?"

"The church elders want us there in two weeks. You know how it is; there will be a lot of meetings, suppers, families to meet."

"I like rural people, they are 'real' people."

"Me too, that is, most of them."

Ruth had been planning and doing some packing. Now she and Jake really got down to business. Mentally Ruth had been deciding what to keep and what to throw away. "Jake, you go through your things. I've been collecting cardboard boxes for some time, you will find plenty on the back porch. There is one thing about it, you'll find you have many mementos. I'm not saying you should throw these away. As time passes some of them will hold very dear memories, especially your graduation day, I think you should keep those."

"OK, Mother." Jake spent the rest of the day sorting one pile he would pack and another pile he would throw away. When he called a halt, true to his mother's observations, it had been hard for him to throw away anything. "Hey, Mom, you were right. I didn't realize so much had happened since we moved here."

"I know. Would you call your father? Supper is ready."

"I hope you cooked a lot of food, because I'm hungry."

"Steak, potatoes, and cream gravy; will that be enough?"

"Sounds good to me."

It seemed good to be back at the family table; the familiar sounds, saying grace, the manner in which his father and mother treated each other. It was so peaceful, so stable. He realized that he was a very fortunate young man.

"How did you two come along with the packing?" asked Jacob. "I'm sorry that I can't help, but my doctor said not to do any lifting or heavy exertion."

Ruth had an answer ready, "Don't worry, we'll have everything packed in two or three days. I'm anxious to get into our house in Big Bend, and I want to see all of the church people."

"And your parents, of course."

"Yes, it will be good to see them. It seems like a long time, although it was only last summer that we visited them."

The rest of the week was spent packing, eating and sleeping. Jake had rented a large U-Haul truck, along with a loading dolly. One afternoon one of the neighbor men had come over to help with the furniture. As was the custom, he had stayed over for supper. He didn't expect any pay, and would have been offended if any had been offered. Neighbors in this part of the country always helped each other. He stayed on for ahile talking about the safe topics; such as the weather, crops, the price of cattle. There was never a word of gossip, it simply was not done. Only God knew if some of the men had broken their vows on occasion, met some gal in a dark corner of a cafe. The womenfolk tolerated small indiscretions, but they would not tolerate their men sleeping around. God knows they could understand how a man could become bored with life.

As their neighbor was leaving he said, "I want to tell you folks we will miss you. It won't be the same. My woman said to tell you the neighbors are planning a pot-luck supper this Sunday evening before church. Is that alright with you?"

"That would be nice."

On Sunday people came from all around, some brought gifts. That evening the church was full. Jake's father was at his best, his sermon was about love and caring. As the people drifted out, they expressed the joy of being together, and sadness over the departure of Jacob's family. there was much hugging and kissing.

One of the neighbor girls, who looked to be about sixteen, cornered Jake. "I'm sorry to see you go, Jake. I can't help but tell you I have always been in love with you."

"I'm sorry, I didn't know."

"When you came to our house, all you could talk about was cars, horses and crops. You know?"

"I'm a fool for not noticing you. I didn't realize you had grown up. I always thought of you as a little girl, a sister."

"Let me tell you, Jake, I'm not your sister. I'm old enough to be your girl, maybe your wife." With that, she grabbed Jake and smothered him with kisses. Breaking off, she ran to a waiting pickup. Jake could see her father at the wheel.

"Well I'll be, I'm sure some kind of fool. That girl has grown up and I didn't realize it."

After the last family had departed, Jake's family returned home. His mother said, "It's time for bed, we have to up early tomorrow. We want to be on the road by six. Mrs. Weeks is coming over to clean up our dishes and things. She'll lock up and keep the key."

"I'm really tired," said Jacob. "Good night."

"Mom, I'll drive the U-Haul tomorrow. You can handle the pickup, can't you?"

"You know I can."

"Good night."

It was still dark when his mother shook him, "Breakfast is ready."

This morning his father's prayer was short, "Oh God, we thank you for this food and our friends. Be with us on our trip. Amen."

Breakfast over, they got into their assigned trucks. Mrs. Weeks was standing on the porch. "Have a safe trip, and God bless all of you. Don't worry, I'll clean up." There were tears in her eyes as she waved good-bye. "Shucks, here I am a grown woman crying like a baby. I'm sure going to miss those folks, they are my kind of people."

On checking the road map, Jake decided to take the turnpike between Oklahoma City and Tulsa. This would shorten their travel time and put them in Tulsa about lunch time. At Tulsa they turned north on highway 75. It was a new cement road with wide shoulders, a pleasure to drive on. After covering about ten miles Jake noticed a secondary road with signs for food and gas. Jake signaled his mother, and they pulled off. After filling up the tank of the truck at a self-service pump, he motioned for his mother to drive up to the same pump. Then they drove over to the cafe, parked and went in.

"How are you doing, Dad?"

"I'm alright, a little tired. With some food and coffee, I'll be alright."

"Are you sure?"

"Yes, I'm sure."

The food, along with the break in the driving, had revived

everyone. They felt that, with the early start, they were over the hump. Getting back into their vehicles, their spirits were high, their hearts were singing. The road to Bartlesville was straight as an arrow. Broad acres of pasture land were all around them, fat herford cattle were busy grazing on bluestem grass. On leaving Caney, Kansas the road suddenly changed to two lanes. Jake stayed on this road till they got to Independence, from there on the road was new to him. From Independence they went to Cherryvale. During their lunch break his mother had said, "We turn right at a small town called, Earlton, then Big Bend is just this side of Shaw. It's so small there is only a fourth-class post office. The church and property are in that vicinity." It wasn't hard to follow his mother's instructions. In about an hour's time he pulled up to a white church.

There was a large group of people waiting. Relatives as well as church members were anxious to see each other. Among the group was Ruth's family. It was a loving event, with sounds of delight, hugging and kissing. Ruth knew most of the people, and was busy introducing them to Jacob and Jake. After everyone had been introduced, there was a pause, then someone announced, "Your house is all ready to move into." Jake drove the U-Haul to the house and lowered the tailgate. The men started unloading the furniture and boxes.

"Ruth, come in the kitchen, the womenfolk redecorated it." Ruth was stunned, the kitchen was a dream; bright colors, new appliances, everything new.

"Joy, come here, I want you to meet our new preacher's wife." A very attractive girl entered the kitchen. "Mrs. Hawkins, I would like you to meet Joy Roberts."

"I'm happy to know you, Joy."

Ruth knew that Joy Roberts was special. She was a beautiful girl with lovely eyes and auburn hair.

"Now let's all go over to the church for our supper." Ruth walked over with Mrs. Hollman and Joy. Jake entered the church looking for his mother. "Jake this is Mrs. Hollman, and this is Joy Roberts. She lives with the Hollmans."

"Yes, I know."

"You know?"

"I mean, she really is a joy, or should be, to know."

"Joy, show Jake where the people are lining up to eat," Mrs.

Hollman said. "And Jake, you are supposed to eat at the head table." But both ladies could see that he wasn't interested in the special table. "Alright, you two can eat anyplace you like. I think I see a table in the corner by door."

Joy and Jake filled their plates with fried chicken, cream gravy and biscuits, along with a glass of Kool-aid. Joy said, "You really don't have to eat with me if you don't want to."

"Believe me, I do." For some reason they were both at a loss and the conversation was slow getting started. "Tell me, Joy, what do the young people do around here for entertainment?"

"Well, since we live in the country, we don't see a lot of the townsfolks."

"Tell me about yourself."

"There isn't much to tell."

"Whatever. I want to hear all about you."

"I've lived with the Hollmans since last year. Actually, my home is in El Reno, Oklahoma. I didn't leave on the best of terms with my parents. You know, it has always been hard for me to talk about my home in El Reno, but you don't seem nosey like most of the people around here."

"You don't have to tell me if it hurts."

"I know it sounds strange, but the Hollmans saved my life."

"Your life?"

"Not exactly, but in a way they did. You see, I ran away from home, I just headed north. One day I walked into their front yard, tired and hungry."

"Gee, you were brave."

"Not really, just lucky, in a way."

"What happened?"

"The same old thing. I thought my parents were too strict. I just headed out, after a stormy session."

"Do your folks know where you are?"

"No, they don't. You see, the Hollmans had lost their daughter in a car wreck. When I walked into their yard, well, Mrs. Hollman said it was an answer to her prayers. She just naturally wanted someone to love."

"You're really something."

"When I first came, we went to the sherrif's office and reported to him. Since I was over eighteen I could do as I pleased, so here I am. Don't you tell anyone around here, I don't want them to know."

"Oh, I won't."

"Now, what about you."

Jake told her about his life at Riverside and his friend, Robert Gombi, but nothing about Mary Marie Tinker.

"Hey, you're a nice looking guy, what about girlfriends?"

"Oh, I've known a few girls, but nothing special."

Joy looked at him, not quite believing what he had said. "No special girl?"

"Nothing."

"OK, it's really none of my business, but you look too good to be free."

"How about you?"

"Nothing. The boys around here don't take to me."

"Boy, they must be blind."

"Oh, I've dated a few of them, but they only want one thing." She paused, looked down, and continued quietly, "They wanted to end up in a cheap motel for a one-night stand. I tell you, Jake, that's not for me."

"I can't say I blame you. A beautiful girl like you doesn't need to sell out cheap."

"Thanks. Hey, everyone is through. I think they are going to ask your father to make a speech."

Sure enough, the deacon in charge stood up and said, "Folks, how about a few words from brother Hawkins?" Everybody clapped.

It was easy for Jake's father to talk, he had nothing but love in his heart for this new church. After the speech the church ladies began picking up the plates and leftovers.

Jake looked straight at Joy, " How about me coming over tomorrow evening?"

Joy smiled slightly, "OK, I would like that."

Both Jake and Joy went home very light-headed, with a song in their hearts.

4

Jake knew that Joy was interested in him. And he still thought about Mary Marie Tinker occasionally but he felt he would never make it with her. He didn't know what it was, something just didn't mesh. What he really wanted to do was meet some more Indian girls.

While he was resting after a day's work he got to daydreaming. His father noticed and asked, "What have you got on your mind, son?"

"I was just thinking about going to Oklahoma. I'd like to see some of my Riverside friends, I miss them. Some of them might be at the American Indian Exposition, if I could go to that."

"My old classmate, Lee Toyebo, lives there, and I think he has something to do with the Fair this year. I'll write to him tonight and see if he can put you up in his camp."

"Thanks, Dad, I would appreciate it." His mind was full of exciting plans. And this would answer a big question: did he want to follow the path of the white man or the Indian? He had to settle this for himself.

He worked hard for the farmers in the neighborhood during June and July, crossing off each day on a big calendar in the kitchen. The Exposition would begin on August the eleventh, and would last a full week, ending on Saturday with a big parade. He would go in the volkswagon his father had given him. He had saved over three hundred dollars, so he could pay for the gas and other expenses.

One evening about dusk he drove over to Joy's, he wanted to talk to someone his own age. As he drove up he saw her in the front yard cutting the grass.

"Hi, Joy, how about going for a ride?"

"That would be nice."

Joy got in and they headed toward town. They stopped at the second drive-in, the place where most of the bucks took their girls. They ordered, and while they were waiting Jake said, "I'm going to Oklahoma about August the ninth to see the American Indian Exposition in Anadarko. I'm going to make camp with a family that my father knows."

Joy listened to Jake, but didn't say anything.

"What's the matter, Joy, you seem so quiet this evening?" He leaned over and looked her squarely in the face. Jake noticed that the farm work had firmed her body and the sun had given her a lovely tan. She looked very beautiful this evening, sitting in the shadow. "Why don't you make the trip with me and see your family in El Reno?"

"We didn't part on the best of terms, I don't know if they would want to see me."

"Why don't you try?"

"I'll let you know. I want to do some thinking about it."

They talked some more, then as Jake was leaving, he said, "Let me know when you decide."

Jake felt they had something in common; they were both outsiders. Jake's father had talked to him many times about the people of Big Bend. "Son, most of the people in this town have preconceived ideas about Indians. You are half Indian, so people will probably call you a breed, or some other name. Don't pay any attention to them, they're ignorant, and are trying to make up for what they don't know. They have ideas about how Indians should act."

"Where did they get these ideas."

"Most of the whites were brought up in the pioneer spirit of getting all they could from the Indians for nothing. Then it began to bother them that they were either trying to kill the Indians or run them off of their land. So the Indian has become a thorn in their conscience."

"Why do some of the whites call me, Chief?"

"It's a way of trying to put you down."

86

"Why would they want to do that?"

"It's hard to explain. It's sort of a protective device. The majority race uses it against any minority they resent. Anything that doesn't belong to their flock, is out. Animals do the same thing. Did you ever watch a bunch of chickens pecking on a weak one? It's sort of a built-in protective device."

"You know, Joy doesn't have this feeling. You can always tell if people have this feeling about you."

"Yes, son, you can."

"Where did Joy lose this feeling?"

"She lost it because she, too, is an outsider."

"She's white."

"Yes, but the townspeople don't accept her, so she feels that she doesn't really belong."

"Then, this is why we understand each other."

"Yes."

"I thought maybe she was feeling sorry for me."

"I doubt it. You might ask her, but she probably doesn't know herself."

"Dad, did you know that Joy is from Oklahoma?"

"No, how do you know?"

"She told me, she is thinking of going to her hometown when I go to the American Indian Exposition."

"That would be nice."

"I think she would like to go home, but she wants to be accepted as a person, not just as a daughter. I sort of hope she'll go home just to find out for herself."

"Yes, it might work out."

"Dad, I have to get some things in town, do you need anything?"

"No, thanks."

"Well, I won't be long."

Jake had seen a hand-tooled billfold in the window of the Saddle Shop. It cost fifteen dollars, which was a little high, but he wanted it for his trip to the exposition. As he was leaving the shop he ran into a boy from their church, "Hi, Bill"

"Hi, Jake."

Jake was somewhat surprised, because he expected to be called, Chief. He conceded that whites were not all alike.

After the chores were all completed, Jake told his father that

87

he was going over to see Joy but would't stay too long.

As he drove up he saw Joy sitting on the front steps. "How did you know I would be over tonight?"

"I didn't know, maybe I had a feeling you might."

Jake sat down beside her. After awhile he asked, "Have you made up your mind about going home?"

"Yes, I have. I wrote a letter today telling them that I would be coming home, and that I would be riding with you. They probably will think that you are my boyfriend,"

"What did you tell them?"

"I told them why I left in the first place and my feelings about the way they treated me. I also told them I wanted to be treated as a person, and didn't want to hear any long lecture about all of the things they had given me."

"What do you think they will say?"

"I will just have to wait and find out, I really don't know. I hope they have changed, but I doubt it."

For her sake, Jake hoped they had written off all the bad things. He couldn't understand how children could become alienated from their parents. He always felt close to his parents. They seemed to understand him; they didn't push him, but were there when he needed them. He had a deep feeling for Joy and wondered how she felt about him, but he wouldn't push it. He knew that Joy had been hurt, she was on guard against the world.

Joy really didn't want to become involved in anything. She was aware that she was spending too much time daydreaming. Mrs. Hollman always had something for her to do, and most of the time it was physical labor, so she didn't have too much time to feel sorry for herself. Farm life had agreed with her, she looked beautifully healthy. Mrs. Hollman liked to sew for her, it helped ease the loss of her daughter. When she went to town the boys looked at her, and she knew why they were looking. None of them had ever called at the farm home, or approached her at church, and this was about the only opportunity that she had to meet young men.

The day finally arrived when Joy heard from her parents. They would welcome her home. They also wrote to ask Jake to spend the night on his way to Anadarko. This was very good news, she felt like a big load had been lifted off of her shoulders. She felt like a different person. She looked in the mirror to see if it show-

88

ed, she thought she saw a new smile, or maybe it was the old one.

Jake's father had heard from Mr. Toyebo who told him where he would be camping and how to get there. He was going t set up camp early. This pleased Jake as it would give him a place to stay while he looked around Anadarko before the exposition started.

The night before they were to leave, Jake went over to Joy's to give her the time of departure. They were engrossed in conversation when they noticed Mrs. Hollman in the background. "When you two get through talking, I want you to come in and have some refreshments."

"OK, we'll be right in."

Mrs. Hollman served them a dish of ice cream. "Are you kids all packed and ready to leave in the morning?"

"Yes."

"Joy, I want you to know it will be mighty lonesome without you. You certainly have been a lot of help to us. We hope you will be back, the door is always open."

"Thanks, you have been so kind to me. I hate to leave, but I have to find out a few things for myself."

"I know, everbody has to find their place in the world. Still I will miss you two, always sitting on the porch talking. Of course, Jake will be back."

"I plan to."

They talked for awhile, said their good-byes, and Jake was on the road home. Neither slept well that night, their anticipation was too exciting.

Early the next morning Jake ate a quick breakfast and said good-bye to his family. When he got to the Hollmans, Joy was all ready to go. Jake could see that Mrs. Hollman was doing her best to keep from crying. She was a strong woman, not one to let her emotions get in her way, but Joy had meant so much to her.

"Would you take my things out to the car, Jake?"

Jake was glad that he had something physical to do, he hated good-byes. He knew that Joy and Mrs. Hollman had been special to each other. Because Jake was in a hurrry to leave, it helped them hurry through the strain of parting.

"Good-bye, good-bye." They went off waving.

Now they were rolling down the road. Joy made small talk for awhile. she felt drowsy, and before long she was asleep. Jake smiled, she seemed completely relaxed. They stopped twice to get something to drink. They arrived in El Reno early in the afternoon. Joy was wide-eyed now as she directed Jake to her home.

When Joy knocked on her front door, her mother answered. "Hello, Joy." They didn't know what to do or say, they were awkward in each other's presence. Finally, Joy put her arms around her mother and gave her a big hug. This surprised Mrs. Roberts, but Jake saw that she was pleased and relieved.

Jake didn't want to stay, he wanted to be on the road again. He got all of Joy's things out of the car. They insisted that he stay for a sandwich and a coke, and to his surprise, he enjoyed it.

It was only about an hours drive from El Reno to Anadarko. When he reached the outskirts of town he pulled over to the side of the road to read his instructions. They said, turn right at the Southern Plains Indian Museum, then turn right again at the arch. Jake didn't have far to go as the arch wasn't far from the stop sign. As he entered the grounds, he noticed numerous tents, brush arbors and RV's. He was directed to Mr. Toyebo's camp by a young Indian girl about his age. He notice that she was much darker than he, with long, jet black hair and brown eyes. She was dressed in jeans and a blouse, with sandles. "This is Mr. Toyebo's camp," she said, then turned and walked away without looking back. Jake watched her until she was out of sight.

"You like her looks?"

Jake turned around and faced a middle-aged man with gray hair creeping up the side of his head. He was a man striking in stature.

Jake was embarrassed, "You see, she was so attractive I didn't thank her."

Mr. Toyebo reached out his hand, "Welcome to camp. How is your father?"

"Oh, he's fine. I think he would have liked to come with me, but he couldn't make it. We left here soon after I graduated from Riverside, and I wanted to come back and check things out."

"I've got to go now, but I'll be back soon, Just make yourself at home. Look around, if you like, you might find some more pretty girls."

As Jake stepped out of the arbor, all he could see in any direction was a mass of tents and arbors. There were some young people around, but no one he recognized. He looked for the girl who

90

directed him to his camp. After awhile he wasn't sure he could tell her from any of the other girls; it didn't keep him from looking. he noticed that a good many of the older Indians spoke in their own language. There were many tribes at this camp; Kiowas, Comanches, Wichitas, Apaches, Caddos, and a few Cherokees and Choctaws from eastern Oklahoma. There were also a few Navajos and Pueblos from various villages in New Mexico.

Before he knew it he had wandered to the extreme south end of the camp. He wasn't sure he could find his way back, but he had been careful to notice the direction he took. He saw the girl he was looking for helping her mother put up a brush arbor. As he came closer, the girl turned and gave him a half smile, he considered this an invitation to her camp. "Hello, I wanted to thank you for helping me find Mr. Toyebo's camp. my name is Jake, I don't believe I got your name."

"Mother, this is the young man I was telling you about. He's staying in Mr. Toyebos camp."

Her mother asked, "Are you related to Mr. Toyebo?"

"No, my father went to school with him. They've been friends for a long time. I went to school at Riverside, but I live in Big Bend, Kansas now."

"My name is Beverly Ross, and this is my mother, Edith."

Jake smiled, relieved that he had been tentatively accepted.

"Come on in, we are putting up our arbor. You can help us."

"I'll be glad to help you. What can I do?"

"All of the large branches must be tied in place before they dry out, or they'll become too hard to handle." Beverly showed him how to use the bark strips. They had been soaked in water and were very flexible. They had worked for about two hours when Jake decided he should go. He was pleased that he would have a place to visit, and someone to show him around that was his own age.

"May I see you tomorrow?"

"If you want to."

"I sure do."

Jaker headed back to where he thought Mr. Toyebo's camp was located. He noticed that even more tents were up, he had to pick his way through them. About the time he thought he was lost, he saw Mr. Toyebo standing by his arbor. "Hello. I thought I would fix us something to eat."

"Good, I wanted to see the south end of the camp. I think I can find my way around now."

"Did you find the girl you were looking for?"

Jake felt a flush coming across his face, "Yes, I did."

"How would you like a pan fried steak?"

"That would be great."

Mr. Toyebo had a camp stove in the arbor that was fueled by butane.

"I thought Indians cooked over an open fire."

"Some of them do, generally older people who have more time, but I have too many things to do."

Jake noticed an electric refigerator. "You have all of the modern conveniences."

"Yes, the old folks have their way, I have mine. There are a lot of flies, and dysentary is pretty common aroung here. Watch what you eat and what you drink.

"I didn't think of that."

"You see, there is little sanitation here. Sometimes the water is kept in containers that aren't always clean."

The evening was full of noises. Jake was used to the noises around a small town and in the country. This was completely different. He could hear the sound of tinkling bells, and someone off in the distance was beating a drum. The wind was light, but it was bringing in the fragrance of wood burning, he could smell the smoke from many camp fires.

He had made a place to sleep by using fresh willow leaves and small twigs. Over this he put his sleeping bag. He laid down to try out his bed while he waited for Mr. Toyebo to come back. He wanted to tell him he was going for a walk. Soon he heard footsteps.

"What do you think of camp life?"

"I like it, this is what I've been looking for."

"Did you get enough to eat?"

"Yes, plenty."

"My wife and the rest of the family will be here day after tomorrow, then you can get some woman cooking."

"How many do you have in your family?"

"The wife and two boys, Joe and Bob. You going walking around this evening?" he asked with a grin.

"Yes, I think I will."Jake was actually very anxious to go over to Beverly's.

"How do you like Beverly?"

"I like her fine. I notice she doesn't have an Indian name."

"Don't pay any attention to the name, it doesn't mean anything. Most all of us have two names, an English name and an Indian name. It all came about when the school teachers couldn't pronounce the Indian names, so they gave us all English names. Now most Indians give their children two names."

Jake fussed around for awhile, he didn't want to appear too anxious to go, although he was. Finally Mr. Toyebo said, "Why don't you go on, Jake? She won't wait around too long for you."

"You are probably right."

Jake had a good idea where Beverly's camp was located now, and it didn't take him long to find it. She was helping her mother with the dishes.

"Hello, may I come in?"

"Hi, come on in. You can help with the dishes."

"It won't be the first time."

"No, you can't help with the dishes, I was only kidding you. If you want to learn how to be a real Indian, this is the first lesson. No Indian man ever helps in the kitchen."

"Mr. Toyebo cooked our supper, and he's a good cook."

"Mr. Toyebo can get away with things no other man can. You see, he is head of the tribal council, and everybody looks up to him. No one would dare poke fun at him. Oh, a few young boys carry out the trash to help their mother, but your young Indian friends would laugh at you. You would be shamed out."

"But at home I often Help my mother."

"That's nice. I understand, but these people wouldn't."

"Well, that's lesson number one."

Beverly put up the cooking utensils, then called, "Mother, I'm going for a walk."

"Alright, but don't stay too long. We still have some work to do."

They walked out into the night. They could see the smoke from many camp fires.

Jake asked, "Where can we go to talk?"

"Let's go to the grandstand."

"The what?"

"Over there is the grandstand where they have the horse

races and the pageant. We can go to the top, hang our legs over the ledge and look at the entire camp. It is always quite a sight."

"Have you been there before?"

"Yes, I've been coming here since I was a little girl. You didn't ask, but I know you are curious about whether I've been here with boys before. The answer is yes, I have a friend in the armed forces. I like him a lot, but we are not engaged or anything."

Jake sighed with relief. When they came to the grandstand, they climbed up and up. The rows of seats were now empty, but soon they would be used by the thousands of people who came every year just to see the Indians. Beverly led Jake to the top step and showed him where to sit to see the entire camp. They put their arms on the railing and looked into the night.

"What do you do when you're not camping?"

"I go to school."

"Where do you go?"

"I'll go to the University of Oklahoma next fall."

"Gee, that's good. What is your major going to be.?"

"Sociology."

"What do you plan to do with your education?"

"Any job that is related to working with Indian people. I think I would like to help the young people understand this world they live in a little better."

The evening was a mixture of talk about school and about camp life. Jake was full of questions, yet didn't want to appear nosey. Beverly might resent so many questions. He screwed up his courage and asked, "How do you like being Indian?"

Beverly was fast to answer, "I wouldn't want to be anything else."

"I'm glad to hear you say that. You are a credit to your race, you know so much about Indians."

"I didn't have to study Indian culture because it has been a part of me ever since I can remember. The Indian way is the only way, as far as I am concerned. Don't get me wrong, I love part of the White man's way."

"Do the white boys treat you good?"

"If they don't, I don't have anything to do with them. I've had some trouble with young men who didn't treat me right. I guess most girls have had their share of experiences with men who want their and nothing more. They don't bother me much. I mind my own

94

business and they soon get the message."

"You were telling me yesterday about the duties of the man. I am ready for a second lesson."

"Oh, yes. The second lesson is more general, it's about how Indians feel toward each other, and how they feel about the world around them."

"That should be interesting."

"First of all, Indians are people; they have the same emotions, feelings, tensions, as everybody else. Indians have a sub-culture of their own, the weddings, the funerals, the honoring of their children. Loved ones are special to Indians. The honoring of individuals is a tribal thing. The give-away after the funeral is important, especially to the older people. They always honor the dead with a dinner and give-away."

"What is your tribe?" Jake asked

"I'm on the Kiowa roll, but my father was Caddo."

Jake thought Beverly was a beautiful young woman with her brown eyes, dark skin, and long black hair. She was small in stature and her features were striking, as if chiseled by a diamond. Jake admired the way she acted and talked, and the amazing amount of information she had given him. Not many girls he had gone to school with could hold a candle to her.

"I wish all Indian girls were like you."

"We are good and bad, just like the rest of the girls in the world. Some do not have any pride, others have, and are trying to make something of themselves. Like the non-Indian girls, they come in all sizes and shapes, with all sorts of ideas. They are moulded by the culture in which they find themselves."

"Yes, I know, but you don't seem to be like most of the girls I know."

"Do you tell that to all the girls?"

"No, only the very special ones like you."

"Do you have a special girl at home?"

"No, but I have a good friend." Jake found himself telling Beverly about Joy, how he thought they were alike in many ways, and how they were different, especially in their relationship with their family.

"Indians tend to feel obligated to take care of their kinfolks. They must do this, as it is a part of saving face. Are you ready for lesson number three?"

95

"Yes, I find this very interesting."

"A lot of non-Indians believe that the Indian is ashamed of his culture. This is what I call a myth. All of the Indians I know think they are God's chosen people. I never did see an Indian who didn't think he was top dog. Non-Indians base success on material things, we base it on our family and friends. Most of the white men work as if they are going to take everything with them when they die, the Indian knows better. The Indian has lived close to the land, his total background has been in harmony with nature. Look around here at the campers, they enjoy the ground, they only want to use it, not own it. This ends the lesson for tonight. Perhaps we can talk again tomorrow evening"

There was a long stretch of silence as they watched the scene below. Finally Beverly turned and smiled. "It's time to go, my mother will worry if I spend too much time away from our camp."

"Do you suppose your mother likes me?"

"Yes I think she does. If she didn't she wouldn't let me go in the first place. Mother prides herself on her knowledge of young men."

"Will she let you go out with white boys?"

"Yes, but I know from the way she acts that she prefers Indian boys. I find I usually like Indian boys best. We seem to understand each other better. How about you?"

"There are some Indians in northeastern Kansas around Horton, but they don't seem like real Indians, they have intermarried so much. I understand they have their own dances and practice the drum religion."

"What kind of religion is that?"

"Most of their religious beliefs are centered around a sacred drum. They believe that when played, the songs will bring good fortune and health to those who listen."

"Do they really believe that?'

"When you get down to the bottom of the barrel, you will believe most anything. This is a way for them to keep their sanity. If it works, I guess it's as good as anything else that people do to keep afloat. They don't get along too well with the whites, and yet a lot of their tribal members have married white men and women. I really think they are oriented toward the old ways. This has helped them in some ways, and in other ways it has been a stone around their neck.

Beverly said, "I hadn't heard about their sacred drum."

After awhile they wandered back to Beverly's camp. They stood for awhile talking about nothing, mostly they were thinking about each other. Beverly was the one to break the long silence, "I have to go in, I'll see you tomorrow."

Jake went on back to Mr. Toyebo's camp, by now he knew the way. He was still fascinated by the relationship among the campers, they seemed to be so much at home.

"How did you make out tonight? Do any better than last night?" Mr. Toyebo asked with a smile.

Jake spoke slowly, "She is a real nice girl, and is real bright. A man would have to work hard to keep in step with her."

"That you would, and you would also have to keep step with her mother."

"What do you mean?"

"Indian mothers are not like white mothers, they sort of take over the girl's family when she marries. That's one reason they are so selective about the man she marries, they will be living with him too."

"I didn't know that it would be like that."

"That's the Indian way."

"How did that custom start?"

"When Indians traveled as tribes or in large bands, certain rules were developed for the protection of all tribal members. If you are around people too much, friction often developes, so they had a rule that the mother-in-law should not speak to the son-in-law. It kept them apart and prevented friction."

"Does this custom still hold?"

"Only with the older Indians. If you move to a city to take a job, you would be on your own, but if you live around here you will have to follow the practice. This is one reason many young couples move to the city, the rules are different."

"In the white culture there are different rules for different parts of the country."

"This is right, however, Indians do the same thing. Each tribe has its own set of rules. If you marry into another tribe you will be working with two sets of rules. It's a little confusing sometimes."

"How about you, do you find the rules binding?"

"Not too much. I realize we must live in the world in which we find ourselves. My wife is well educated, and so we see pretty

97

much eye to eye. I like the Indian ways, and I respect them, but they don't always work for me."

While they were talking Jake noticed a group coming toward their camp. Mr. Toyebo noticed them too, "It looks like my wife and the rest of the family." They arrived all smiles.

"This is my wife, Esther, and my sons, Joe and Bob."

They all extended their hands, the grasp was only a touch. Jake remembered that Indians consider it rude to grab the hand and shake it hard. Jake knew that he was going to enjoy this family. They seemed so very warm, but they were also poised and full of dignity. The evening was spent with the Toyebo family, telling and retelling stories about the past two days.

The next day Jake went over to Beverly's. He wanted to make plans for the evening. Beverly had gone to town, so Jake spent the rest of the morning walking around. He went over to the racetrack where there was much activity. That afternoon the races would begin, now the trainers were working out their horses. The concession men were getting ready to sell their wares.

Jake stood around for awhile, then went back to Beverly's. She had returned from town and when she saw him coming, she looked very happy.

"Hello, Jake, I've been to town, Have you been over here before?"

"Yes, I came this morning, but your mother said you had gone to town."

They spent the rest of the day just looking around and talking. Beverly showed him where various relatives and friends were camping. They went in and talked to some of them. Jake was a few Riverside students, but none that he knew well.

Beverly invited Jake to stay for supper to have some camp stew. He had eaten stew before, but this was a new experience, actually it was just boiled meat. He watched Beverly's mother dip her bread into the juice and bring it up to her mouth in one stroke. She had had a lot of practice.

The carnival had not been set up yet so they just sauntered around and made small talk. Jake spent most of his time looking at Beverly. Once she caught him; she grinned and ducked her head. By the time they returned to her camp, the night was pleasantly cool after the hot day.

"It's time to come in, Beverly."

Beverly responded, "Yes, Mother." There was no bickering over the request, she knew what was expected of her.

"Goodnight, Jake, I'll see you tomorrow. Everyone will sleep late tomorrow."

Jake realized that although everone was polite to him, they didn't consider him an Indian, they considered him an outsider. The wonder of it was that Beverly seemed to treat him as a good companion. It was strange, he was an Indian but he felt like an alien.

The next morning Jake walked slowly toward Beverly's camp. He was not too anxious to face Beverly, and yet he wanted to talk to her and ask her so many things. When he got there he could hear Beverly talking to her mother. They must have heard him too, for about that time Beverly stuck her head out of the arbor, all smiles. Jake wondered if this was just for him, but he knew that Beverly was not likely to be carried away so easily.

Beverly had given more thought to Jake than he supposed. In her own way she had weighed all of the possibilities. What if Jake wanted to know about her future plans? She had told him about her boy friend in the armed forces, but he had been gone so long that he didn't mean a lot to her. She felt that Jake was sincere. She daydreamed about a possible future with him. So this was the reason she gave him a veryl special smile.

Jake appreciated the smile, however he didn't really know what was behind it. He didn't know that girls looked down the road a lot further than boys, that when they were attracted to a man it was as a possible husband. Their role was different, they had to wait to be chosen, and the pretty girl had a much better chance than the plain one. Beverly had been endowed with grace and beauty, enough to turn any young man's head. In a way she had become tired of all the flattery, the stares, and so it was refreshing to have someone like Jake who liked her for herself.

But Jake didn't get to bask in the warm smile for long. Beverly told him she had to rehearse for the pageant, and would see him that evening.

The evening began to take on enchantment as Jake walked towards Beverly's camp. He noticed some dancers who also seem-ed to experience a sense of excitement. Although they were good at masking their feelings, they felt that the dance was more than just a dance. It was an opportunity to show off a new costume, to completely lose themselves in the rhythm of the drums.

Beverly had bought some new jewelry while in New Mexico, and had polished the silver until it gleamed. The turquoise was the best, a blue-green stone. She felt that this would be a special evening. She had dressed with care in her buckskin dress. She was pleased with herself. She also knew that there was something else on her mind, she secretly hoped that it would be on Jake's mind also.

She was ready when Jake called. They walked slowly through the crowd, aware that people were watching them, especially the non-Indians. They realized that they made a handsome couple. Jake wondered if they thought of him as an Indian, but he really didn't care. He felt that he and Beverly were in a special kind of world, a world in which they were the only persons and where nothing else mattered.

Jake left Beverly at the performers' gate with a simple goodbye. She gave him one of her best smiles, and was off for her part in the evening's show. From high in the grandstand Jake searched for Beverly, but couldn't spot her among the dancers. They did not seem to have any special coloring, it was as if they were out of focus and he couldn't really see them. Suddenly an image was closer, it was Beverly. He became alarmed, this couldn't happen to him. He sat there as if stunned, it was five minutes before he moved. Beverly was the one—she had completely won him. He continued to sit there with his head bowed. He felt dizzy, he needed to walk. Leaving the grandstand, he went out on the midway. He took a deep breath and smelled hamburgers and popcorn. People were laughing, little children were squealing. Mothers were chasing the little ones, while the older ones darted away and headed for the sideshow. This bright, loud world around, and Jake was almost totally unaware of it. There were thousands in the grand stand, and almost as many walking around the midway. For about an hour he was a part of the entire panarama. Little did he know that this same drama was happening to other young men who had found their true love at the American Indian Exposition.

He continued walking, looking, but not seeing. He bought a hamburger but did not taste it. He bumped into people on the midway, some made remarks to him, he didn't hear them.

Jake finally realized he should return to the grandstand and pick up Beverly. He went to the Indian gate, since the performance was almost over, the gatekeeper had left. He found a small box and stood on it so he could see Beverly.

She was one of the first performers to come out. Beads of sweat covered her forehead, and her face was flushed. When she saw Jake she smiled, it wasn't an eager smile, but a tired one.

"Let's get out of here. I'm about to drop."

Jake took her by the hand and didn't waste any time getting back to her camp. "I'll see you in about five minutes." She disappeared behind the curtain of her tent.

When she came out, it was a different Beverly, she looked cool and rested. "Let's walk," she said as she reached for Jake's hand. They headed for their favorite spot, the grandstand. They dangled their legs over the ledge and gazed at the crowd below them.

"The crowd doesn't change any from year to year," Beverly said. "I guess some of the faces change, but they look the same. What do you think of the Indians here?"

Jake's answer did not come quickly. He remembered thinking that the Indians he had seen camping here didn't have much in common with Mary Marie and Darla. But he had seen Indians in the grandstand tonight who looked just like them. "I still have a lot to learn, I'm sure of that, but you have taught me a lot. If they were all like you I'd feel that I knew them better."

Beverly was pleaed to hear this, and she smiled her quick, pixie smile that he knew and loved so well.

Jake reached over and held her hand.

"Do you like holding my hand?"

"Yes I do. I think you are about the most perfect girl I have ever known."

Beverly turned and looked him in the face, "You have the exposition madness. When the sounds of drums and the midway fade, your excitement will also change."

This caught him off guard. "Why do you say that?"

"Because I have seen it happen to a lot of girls and boys. They think this is their big moment, only to find out later that it is the exposition madness. Sometimes they marry, sometimes they just start living together—it doesn't last. I think you are sincere, but I don't want to be caught up in it. Wait until next winter and see if you still feel the same way." She reached up and held his

101

head in both of her hands, and kissed him gently. "Until then, let's leave it like it is."

"I am willing to wait until you say the word. I have plenty of time, and you are worth waiting for."

"I think we should go, Mother will wonder what happened to me. She is pretty strict and proud, I wouldn't want to do anything to hurt her."

"I can understand, I think I would be the same way about you."

At the entrance of the arbor she kissed him again.

5

"What will you have, Mac?"

"Bacon and eggs, over easy, with a cup of black coffee."

The air on the midway was filled with the aroma of bacon and coffee. It remided Jake of home and wheat harvest. Heat from the burning sun was a part of summer in Kansas. He loved the harvest season. It was a time for movement, new people, excitement.

The American Indian Exposition was a different world, he mused as he ate his breakfast. There wasn't much going on at this hour.

The old-timers were right when they said it would be this way. All week people stayed up too late, and the next morning they felt exhausted. Beverly was really tired after the pageant, and her mother insisted that she not stay out late.

One afternoon Jake walked to town with her to do some shopping. And every evening he would walk with her from her camp to the grandstand. After the performance he met her at the Indian gate. When she had changed from her buckskin dress to something cooler, sometimes they went to the midway for a cold drink, sometimes to the top of the grandstand.

After his breakfast, Jake felt lonesome and walked over to Beverly's. She seemed different this morning, but she said, "Things haven't changed. We're both tired, I think we need a rest from each other." She kissed him with feeling, smiled, and walked away.

After about an hour of walking around, Jake sat down at a booth selling hamburgers and coffee. He wasn't hungry, but it was someplace to sit and think.

"What's the matter, boy, you sick?"

Jake glanced up, "No, I'm alright."

"Why don't you eat your hamburger?"

"I guess I'm not hungry."

"Why did you order it then?"

Jake didn't say anything. He drank the rest of his coffee, and left the hamburger on a paper napkin. The consession man was still looking at it, muttering. Jake saw him hold it up to his nose.

Jake kept on wandering until he came to the barbed wire fence at the edge of the camp. There was an unusual number of people there. They reminded him of a vulture he had once watched. It just sat on its perch until the animal became isolated from the group, then, with one big swoop, it pounced on it and picked it to death. These people were the same way, they knew something was going to happen and they wanted to be in on it. There would be the usual number of drunk, white men looking for a young Indian girl. It made Jake sick. He knew that, sooner or later, men of all ages would come toward the camp to find themselves a girl. For the most part they would be young, but the drunks wouldn't be so young.

One young, white boy came along with an Indian girl who looked to be about thirteen years old. She was so very young that she spent all of her time giggling with her hand over her mouth. This was too much. Jake went over, threw the boy around, and hit him in the face with his fist. The boy was knocked out, and the girl was so frightened she just stood there, stunned. Finally she started running back toward the carnival grounds, and darted between two tents. Many of these young girls thought it was something they could brag about. It was a form of daring, excitement. The sound of the drums, and the dancing hypnotized them. After it was all over it seemed like a dream.

Now that he had jumped one boy, Jake felt like stalking another. The word had probably traveled fast, so it would be more difficult to find another couple. He had never experienced anything like this before.

Jake sat on an old stump and began to relax. He felt very tired, and had lost all of his energy. He slid down from the stump and leaned against it. Soon he fell asleep. He woke suddenly, his reflexes told him someone was near. His long hours in the country had conditioned him to be aware of noises. He didn't move. Apparently someone thought that he was drunk and they were going to roll him. As Jake grabbed for the man, his hand caught in a pocket and the man slipped out of his jacket and ran toward the crowd. Jake knew that it was useless to try to find him, so he gave up the chase. The sleep and excitement had rested him and cleared his head. He didn't know what time it was as he had left his watch at the camp. He decided to go there and see the Toyebo's.

Jake could hardly believe that this was already Friday and that it was time to meet Beverly at the Indian gate. He shoved his way through the crowd. Some people gave him angry glances, but he was totally unaware of them. There was one thing on his mind, he had to see Beverly. It was like a Roman holiday. Flash cubes on cameras twinkled in the grandstand. Clouds had blown in, reflecting the various lights...it was erie. The evening was hot and the spectators were fanning, their collars open. But no one left early, they were actually a part of the dance, following every beat, hypnotized by the entire scene. Now a long line of dancers was coming through the gate. Finally he saw Beverly. She looked very tired, sweat beads had formed on her face. She didn't say anything, just smiled and reached for his hand. The midway was crowded with people stopping at the concession stands.

Jake left her at the arbor's entrance. He knew that her mother would have a tub of water ready for her to bathe, he could hear her splashing the water over her body. When she appeared, she had on a fresh dress and a ribbon in her hair. He felt like he needed a shower, he actually felt dirty compared to her.

This seemed like a dream to Jake, or a replay of an old record. He had gone through the same experience just the other night, now he was beginning to understand what Beverly meant by the exposition madness. He knew now that Beverly had been very wise, she knew about the madness. Jake was deep in thought, trying to decide what he would say to Beverly. He walked over to her and drew her very close. Her eyes were bright with good humor as if she knew what was about to happen.

"Beverly, I have something I want to ask you."

"Yes?"

"It may be too soon, but since this is almost the end of the exposition, I want to know. Will you marry me?"

Beverly looked down, smiled and said, "You will have to ask my mother."

Jake didn't want this, but he knew it was probably the way it would have to be. "Is your mother in?"

"Yes, but she is asleep. The day has been too long for her, you will have to see her tomorrow."

Jake didn't relish seeing Beverly's mother because he felt that she had certain reservations about him.

Jake and Beverly decided to go to the grandstand again. It was silent and dark, only an hour before it had been covered with humanity and blazing with lights. They climbed to the top of the grandstand and watched the people walking in a circle around the midway. From their vantage point the people looked like a group of bugs. They didn't say a word, but they were both thinking about the same thing. Finally Jake broke the silence, "What if you mother turns me down?"

Beverly didn't say anything for a long time. "You know that I belong to the old Indian school and will have to go along with my mother's wishes."

"Well, I'll just have to present my case the best I know how."

The spell was broken, they both knew that they should return to her camp. They moved slowly down, down until they reached the ground floor. They moved in unison, hand in hand, through the almost deserted midway. At Beverly's camp she reached up and gave him a kiss. "I'll see you after the parade."

Jake returned to his camp and was surprised to find that Mr. Toyebo was still awake.

"Well, have you learned about camp Indians?"

"Yes, I've learned a lot."

"How do you like us?"

"You have your own special ways, but basically you want the same things as other people, only you want it a little different. It's not so unusual."

"And what about the girls?"

"I find them like other girls, only they have different values, and different ways of doing things."

"Any special girl?"

Jake knew that Mr. Toyebo was talking about Beverly. "Yes,

I find Beverly a very special girl. I have asked her to marry me, what do you think of that?"

"What did she say?"

"She said that I would have to see her mother."

"Yes, that's the Indian way alright. You are going to have a tough fight on your hands. Beverly's mother doesn't want to give her up, and she will put you through the wringer."

"What do you think she'll say?"

"I don't know, but don't be surprised if she puts you off for awile. She knows this is a summer romance, but after a little time she might put it to the test of the real thing. Indians are not romantically involved like the white man. They think that any young man, if properly trained, would make a good husband. They place more value on the traits of the individual, his parents, and what they stand for. They are protecting their daughters against what they consider an unfortunate marriage. Marriage is also a financial thing which involves the exchange of gifts between families. She will weigh these things before she gives her consent. Beverly has been raised in this atmosphere, so she will abide by her mother's wish."

The next day the exposition opened full swing, everybody was up early getting ready for the parade. Although the fair was supposed to have been over the night before, the promoters had passed the word around that there would be one more day. Everybody in the parade would receive rations plus a small amount of money. There was a friendly rivalry among the campers for the best float, the best dressed walker, and the largest representative tribal group.

Jake felt the excitement around him, there was a tempo that he used to feel before a football game. He walked toward the center of town. Cars were already parked along the streets, tourists were arriving by the thousands. Hawkers appeared on vacant lots as if by magic at hot dog stands and cold drink stands. There wasn't an empty spot close to town. Busses from Ft. Sill arrived with a marching band. Special excursion buses from Oklahoma City arrived pouring out the passengers into the milling crowd. Many had been there before and had become hooked on the parade, they wouldn't miss it for anything.

Most people knew that it would be hot, and the parade would

be long, so they brought all types of equipment for themselves and their families. They had folding chairs, umbrellas, colored glasses or eye shades, picnic baskets. Older women dressed in their country best, sun bonnets, skirts well below the knee, and sleeves down to the wrist. Girls wore short shorts, peek-a-boo blouses, and large sun glasses. Boys were in jeans, cowboy boots, and straw hats cocked at a rakish angle. Once in a while you would see an Indian boy with a white girl, or the other way around, not often, but it did happen.

The side streets had been blocked off so that cars would not cross in front of the parade. The Wichita float followed the Fort Sill army band. The ladies skirts were long with bright ribbons sewn on them. Most of the riders were girls. They sat on the hood of the car which had been covered with Indian blankets. Men in Indian dress were walking. They didn't consider it manish to sit on the cars like the ladies and the girls.

Jake didn't know enough to tell the difference in the costumes of the tribes, but he wanted to see the Kiowa float because Beverly said she would be riding on it. He had to wait for about half an hour. He enjoyed the clowns that came by in a truck, they were called the mud daubers. The people on the sidewalks gave them a big hand.

Then he saw Beverly. She was sitting on the hood of a car draped with Pendleton Indian blankets. There were also two small children on the car. He hoped that she would recognize him. She had on a beaded buckskin dress and a beaded headdress, she looked regal. The car had almost passed by when Beverly glanced in his direction, she nodded and raised her hand in a half wave, like the queen of England does. He hoped that the gesture was for him, at least he thought it was.

The parade was endless, more and more cars, more high school bands. But for Jake, the parade was over. He now began to watch the people on the sidewalks. It was hot, still people watched until the last car had gone by. Then they gathered up their chairs and their children and went to their cars. They wanted to get out to the exposition grounds as soon as possible. Some of them had become too weary with all the heat, so they headed for home. There were many Indians watching who lived in Oklahoma City or Tulsa. They were proud of this all-Indian affair. The exposition was planned and run by them. The whites had tried to get into the act, but they were treated with indifference.

It was now almost half past two, and Jake realized he had not eaten. The hamburger business was flourishing, and Jake had to wait in line for a soggy hamburger and a bottle of pop. Most of the large families had brought along a picnic basket, and had found some shade.

After he had eaten, Jake hurried out to the exposition grounds. He was tense with excitement. When he arrived at the Toyebo camp they were already back from the parade.

"Hi, Jake, how did you like the parade?"

"I thought it was great."

"Sit down and get something to eat." It was more of a command than an invitation. Jake was still hungry, the hamburger and pop had hardly made a dent in his appetite. The boys still had on part of their costumes and paint on their faces. It seemed rather strange for them to be talking in English with that paint on their faces. The food was good and there wasn't much conversation. Everyone reached a point of satisfaction about the same time. Joe and Bob asked to be excused.

"How do you like camping?"

"I like it fine, but where do people shower and clean up?"

This amused Mr. Toyebo. "There is a wash pan over there, and a five gallon jerri can of water. Wait until it gets dark and take a bath out of the wash pan. It's easy to develop a camp odor; wood smoke, cooking, food, and dust. Some people don't bother to bathe during the exposition, they wait until they get home and go to the creek."

Jake was tired from the heat and the parade, so he decided to lie down on his bedroll until after the races started. When he woke up it was dusk, he couldn't believe he had slept most of the afternoon. He got up, went outside and washed his face. The entire area was covered with a haze of dust and smoke.

There was no one around the Toyebo camp so he decided to go over to Beverly's. In all directions he saw tourists busy taking pictures. Since the August heat had dried up the ground, the thousands of people that were milling about were stirring up dust. Jake had never seen so many people interested in Indians. He hoped they were truly interested and not just here to take pictures.

When he reached Beverly's camp he found they had completely covered the arbor entrance with willow branches. At first

it looked as if no one was there, then he thought he saw movement inside.

"Beverly?"

"Yes."

"It's Jake. Are you alright?"

"Oh, yes. Come on around to the back and come in."

"I thought something was wrong when I saw everything
enclosed."

"No, we are fine. Mother doesn't like the dust or the tourists
looking in. She doesn't like people taking pictures of her or her
camp either. So she just put up a screen to keep out what she
doesn't like. Have you eaten?"

"Yes, I had a little lunch with the Toyebo's about three
o'clock."

"Won't you have something else?"

Jake could tell from the look on Beverly's face that she wanted
him to eat. He didn't want to hurt her feelings so he decided to
eat again.

Beverly's mother had some of her kinfolks in for dinner. She
introduced them all to Jake, then they sat down to eat. The food
was good; pan fried steak, boiled potatoes, sliced tomatoes and
iced tea. No one seemed interested in talking. Once in awhile
someone would say something in Indian, then continue eating.
He wondered what they were saying. Without looking up Beverly's
mother said, "Jake, I want to see you after the show tonight."
Usually Beverly helped with the dishes, but her mother insisted
that they go on.

They looked at the exhibits, bought a balloon, and tried to
win a doll by throwing at milk bottles. They did win a bamboo cane
at the bingo game. They sat down in the shade of a booth that
wasn't being used. After awhile Beverly said, "I'm in the pageant
again tonight, I'll have to go get dressed in a few minutes."

"I'll see you after the pageant."

They walked back to Beverly's camp, talked for a few minutes,
then Jake went on to the Toyebo's camp.

By now the dancers were getting dressed for the pageant.
They all seemed to be in a good humor, they would get paid, but
this wasn't the most important thing. This evening they would get
to dance with their friends, people that they hadn't seen all summer. The dancing would be on an individual basis, they would strut

around and show off their new costumes. There would be a large audience composed mostly of non-Indians, and some Indians who had not camped, but were here only for the evening. All Indians could get in for fifty cents at the Indian gate on the south side. Jake had wondered if he could get in at the Indian gate, but he hadn't had any trouble. They were more interested in getting the money than anything else. The grandstand was already crowded, he found a single seat near the top. The hawkers of cold drinks, hot dogs and peanuts were out in full force. Jake watched the crowd with a great deal of interest. They were well dressed in the current fashion, had cameras, field glasses, and some had tape recorders.

About nine o'clock the drummers came out to the center of the circle and started drumming and singing. Men, women, boys, and girls of all ages came out in costume, or just a shawl. They did a social dance, the women doing their sliding two-step, the men doing different types of dances according to their tribe. The actual pageant didn't start till half past nine. It was called, "Return of the Redman." It started with the old days, then showed that Indians were working in many different jobs. Some were dressed as college students, some in vocational training, some dressed as farmers and technicians. Jake looked for Beverly, but didn't see her. He wished that he had a pair of field glasses. He thought the pageant was amazing; he had never seen anything like it.

When it was all over he went to the Indian gate and waited. In about fifteen minutes Beverly came out. All of the performers were being paid tonight, so she had waited for her money. She had on her beaded buckskin dress, a beaded headband, and bright ribbons trailed down her back. "Let's go over to the camp, I want to change my clothes, this buckskin dress is hot."

Jake was pleased to be so close, he couldn't keep his eyes off of her. he noticed that the people who were streaming out of the grandstand were also looking at her, she looked like a princess. This was the life!

Beverly was definitely in command. She only glanced at Jake as they hurried along. When they entered the arbor she said, "You can wait here, I will go change my clothes." Beverly was an interesting girl, she was all business tonight. Soon she would change from the person in the pageant to a wistful, thought provoking, and very feminine girl. After awhile Beverly came out, she didn't look like the same girl. She was wearing a pair of white slacks and a white blouse.

"Where shall we go, Jake?"

"I would like to walk around and look at people."

"Any special direction?"

"Let's go over to the game of chance first, we might win something."

They played two games of Bingo, but didn't win anything. They tried the magic wheel and won two pins that said ."Kiss me quick!" They pinned them on their clothes, laughing all the while, wondering what they would do if someone really tried to kiss them.

Jake said, "Remember, your mother wants to talk to me."

"Yes, I remember, but let's walk around awhile first."

There was a silence between them as they walked along the crowded carnival grounds. Finally she said, "It's time to talk to Mother."

Jake had mixed feelings about this encounter; elation, fear, wonderment, and most of all, excitement. Up to this time it had always seemed like a long distance to Beverly's camp, now they were there before he knew it. Jake followed Beverly in. Her mother was sitting on a cot. She greeted them, then came directly to the point. "You want to marry Beverly?"

"Yes."

"What do you have to offer? Cattle? Horses?" She paused to see his reaction.

This was all new to Jake, even though he had been warned by Mr. Toyebo. "I don't have any cattle or horses."

"How do you plan to take care of Beverly? Will she live with your folks?"

These very practical questions had not come to Jake's mind.

Beverly's mother pushed on. "What are your habits? Have you known other girls?"

Beverly didn't show any emotion, she sat on a stool with her eyes almost closed, looking at the ground. Not entering into the conversation was a daughter's proper conduct. There was no noise in the arbor, just the distant sounds of the carnival. They sat there for what seemed to Jake like a long time, then the mother spoke, "Young man, come back later when you have your wits collected. In the meantime you may walk with Beverly." Beverly raised her head and smiled, it was over.

112

They walked out of the arbor into the camp grounds. Jake reached for Beverly's hand, they felt alone in the midst of the throngs of people.

Beverly was the first to speak, "Don't worry, everything is alright. Mother really likes you. She has to follow the old custom, all that about horses and cattle was to shake you up. She knows they don't give horses anymore, but she was serious about you getting your plans in order. Let's not worry about it anymore."

Jake was relieved. Beverly reached over and kissed his cheek, they looked each other in the face for several minutes, then they smiled, and the spell was gone.

The night was warm, there didn't seem to be any movement of the air. The crowds milled through the carnival grounds, and as the night wore on they became more restless.

The crowds in the midway and along the roads did not bother the children. They continued to play their games of make believe. Soon they would lie down on their pallets in a tent and go to sleep.

"Jake, I have to go. Mother will be worried about me."

"I know."

Jake stopped, turning to face Beverly. Although surrounded by people, it didn't matter, they stood with their arms around each other. Jake was the first to speak, "I love you so much, I just can't get enough of you. I want to spend all my life with you."

"I love you too, Jake." Only a few people seemed to notice them. "Let's go, I really must get back to our camp."

Hand in hand they moved around the tents, automobiles, trailers, and sleeping people. As they reached her tent, Beverly heard a familiar voice. "Is that you Beverly?"

"Yes, Mother."

"It's late, come to bed."

Beverly looked tired. Jake reached for her and gave her a kiss. "Good night, I'll see you tomorrow." There was no more to be said.

The last night of the exposition was like Las Vegas, no one wanted to leave. The older people began to drop out. Exhausted they returned to their tents. The young, because of their energy, stayed on.

Jake didn't go to the Toyebo camp. He was tired, but he wanted to drink in everything that he saw. This he would remember for a long, long time.

There was a large group of non-Indian boys on the midway looking for females. Some of them found what they were looking for, and walked down the midway with their arm around their pickup, their faces flushed with excitement. Although they were underage, they had managed to get some liquor, mixed it with pop, and given it to the girls. Some of them were staggering, laughing, and making uncontrolled noises while the boys were trying to get them off into the darkness. One girl passed out. Suddenly an Indian policeman showed up, and the boys scattered and ran. The girls were still laughing, and some were crying, some were muddled and fell to the ground. The Indian policeman got some of the Indian adults to help him carry them back to the camp. It was a sad sight.

Peddlers of watermellons were out in force, getting higher prices this week. Two or three little boys threw rocks at the man with watermellons, and while he chased them, other little boys pulled a mellon from his truck.

The games of chance were always a poor risk, Indians stayed away from them. They did like the side shows, the wrestling matches, and the freak shows. When they would come out to give a free performance, the boys would run to the back, lift up the tent, and dart to the ring in the center of the tent. Most of them had money, it was just the idea of getting in free, and beating the white man. Everyone was playing their role, there was little overlapping.

Jake could smell cedar, thrown into a fire to keep the evil spirits away. The evening was finally coming to an end. It writhed, as if it were some large dragon spitting fire, knocking over everything in sight. It had been a disturbing day, those who slept did not sleep in peace, but tossed and turned.

Jake fell exhausted on his bedroll, but his sleep was troubled. He dreamed he was swimmming, the water was so refreshing. He began to move his arms, and woke up. He sat up and looked around, everything was quiet. There was some doubt in his mind about this kind of life, part of it he liked, part of it he didn't. Maybe he had lived another kind of life for too long a time.

when Jake awoke the next morning the sun was shining and it was hot. He looked at his watch, it was almost nine o'clock. The two Toyebo boys were still sleeping, but their parents were gone. Jake decided that he would walk over to the midway and get a

114

breakfast of bacon and eggs.
    The American Indian Exposition had come to an end.

6

Jake returned to the routine of the farm in Kansas. It seemed awfully dull after his week at the American Indian Exposition. He missed Beverly. Joy had not come back with him, she wanted to visit her folks in El Reno for awhile.

During supper Jake noticed that his father was preoccupied. Finally he asked, "What's the matter, Dad?"

"Well, son, I have finally realized that I never will be anything but a country preacher and a small-time farmer. I have watched other preachers move on to bigger churches, move up the ladder, so to speak."

"I didn't think it mattered to you."

"That's what I told myself, but, being a human being, I must admit that I thought I might end up being more than a country preacher. I know what the secret is, but I just can't do it. You have to patronize the men and flatter the ladies, I wasn't cut out for such things. I just like to tell it like it is. But sometimes I feel like a failure."

"Gee, Dad, I thought you had come to like being a country preacher."

"I do, son, I guess the devil had hold of me today."

His father sat there for a long time, then he said, slowly, "If you have any understanding of what I am talking about, you are a man, no longer a boy."

Jake didn't offer any comment. He just sat there until his mother came in. Jake found something he had to do, and his father went out to the barn. Both felt that they needed to be alone. Jake didn't want to face his thoughts. His father didn't want to face the fact that his wife might have something to say about the situation. She might think that he was unhappy with her, all sorts of complications could arise from a simple, honest evaluation.

Jake went out to the pasture to replace some rotten fence posts. At this time of the year the ground was hard and dry, and every time he used the posthole digger it bounced back at him. Jake had to use all of the force he had to get each hole started. Once the upper crust was broken the job was easier. He realized he was digging holes with a frenzy. He stopped to get a drink of water. With the digging had come a relaxing of his mind and muscles, he actually felt rested. Later he thought of Beverly and her mother, and wondered what he was going to do. He worked even harder, but the thought was in the back of his mind, and by the time he returned to the house he felt exhausted. He went out to the well, and pumping some water, he put his head under the faucet. He sat down under a tree and closed his eyes. This was not helping, perhaps a trip to town would change his mood.

As he drove to town he kept thinking of a possible solution. He knew he had to have an answer for Beverly's mother, but what? Jake felt like he had the weight of the world on his back. He would have to ask his father, he always seemed to have the right answer. With this conclusion, Jake felt his problem was solved for the moment. He spent the next hour walking up and down the street. Most of the boys he knew were gone, and the town looked as lonesome as he felt, this hot, summer afternoon.

Joy had come back from El Reno, and Jake wondered how she was working out her problems. Suddenly he saw Joy coming toward him. They both walked faster. It was great to see someone you could talk to, someone who accepted you. Joy had never told anyone else here about her parents in El Reno, so they didn't know that her parents were as well off as anyone in this town. This wasn't really important to her, what she wanted was to be accepted. She felt completely at ease with Jake, they understood each other.

"How are you, Jake."

"Thought I would come to town to catch up on some of the local gossip, however, none of the boys seem to be around. Let's go get a coke."

They walked down to the corner where all of the kids went for something to drink. They found a booth in the back and ordered. They really didn't need to talk, just being together seemed to relax them.

"This would be a good afternoon to swim, how about it?"

Joy's face flushed, she knew what went on at the swimming hole. Jake saw her reaction, "I didn't mean we would have to swim like the others."

Joy laughed, "I know." They sat there for awhile not talking, just thinking. "Do you suppose anybody else would be swimming this afternoon? I would like to go, but I don't want to swim with a lot of others, I don't like their company."

"We could drive out and look, if there were others, we could come on back home."

"Let's go."

They piled into Jake's bug and were off to the swimming hole. It was late August, there wasn't any wind except the breeze that the motion of the car made. Jake parked the car by the lake, and they walked over to the beach. It was shimmering in the hot sun and the water was a deep blue. They walked out to the water's edge. Jake wondered where all of the girls and boys were that usually came at this time of the day.

Suddenly Joy said, "I didn't bring my suit."

"Neither did I. You go over behind those trees and undress and I'll put my things in the car."

Joy hesitated for a moment, but only for a moment, she was behind the trees before Jake got to the car. He wasn't sure this was the right hting to do. If his father heard about it, he sure would be in trouble. Jake heard a car in the distance. He called over to Joy, "Wait a minute, I hear someone coming." Joy put her clothes on in a hurry and got back to the car. They met the other car soon after they got started. They waved, but Joy looked the other way.

Jake took Joy home. They sat in the car for a long time and didn't say anything. Jake was thinking it would have been a good swim, but he was glad he heard the car coming in time to get out of there.

"Thanks anyway, Jake. I'd better go in, it's time I did some work around here."

On the way home Jake worked out a plan he could live with. He decided to go to college--maybe his dad could help him get an educational grant through his tribal council. He would go to see Beverly a week before school started. At school he would have a chance to sift out the details of his life.

That night he dreamed of snakes. They were all around him, he would run and run, but they were still there. He awoke several times terrified. Finally he got up, went to the kitchen, and made himself a sandwich and got a glass of milk. He couldn't shake the awful feeling. What could have caused such a bad dream? He thought he must be sick. He went to the mirror to look at himself; everything seemed to be the same as yesterday.

The next afternoon he and Joy decided to try the swimming hole again. Jake wanted to lie on the warm sand, to bake in the sun. It was great, the summer sun heated him through and through. He laid his arm over his eyes to shade them from the sun and fell asleep. He dreamed again of snakes, but this time there was only one small cobra that raised its head. He recognized a place that he had been in North Dakota. The wind was blowing the prairie grass, his clothing was being torn off of him by the wind. He screamed again and again. He felt the pressure of someone shaking him. When he awoke he was still at the swimming hole, and Joy was shaking him. "Where am I?"

"What's wrong?" Joy had a puzzled look on her face.

"I guess I went to sleep and had a bad dream."

Jake reached up to Joy and pulled her down to him. Neither said anything, they didn't have to. The natural thing to do was to hold each other in a close embrace. Jake closed his eyes, in a deep kiss he felt relaxed. He didn't move, the embrace continued.

Joy felt very deeply about Jake, and when he didn't make any further moves, she was disappointed. When Jake stopped kissing her she rolled over in the sand and gave a long sigh. For some reason this amused Jake and he smiled at her. Jake thought he was probably a dummy for not taking advantage of this situation. He reached for Joy's hand. They stared into the summer sky with white clouds barely moving eastward. The warm sun penetrated their bodies, soaking away any care or worry. A bullfrog began to croak, two crows circled above, cawing. Flies and mosquitoes began to buzz around them. The sun and the insects were too much. Jake grabbed Joy's hand and they ran together to the water. As they reached the water's edge Joy screamed, "I can't go in, I have on my play clothes."

119

"Take them off."

Joy stood with her legs spread in the sand and looked directly at Jake. Jake turned around and ran for the water, leaving Joy standing on the beach. He shed his shorts enroute. It was like a game of checkers. He swam to the center of the lake. It was now Joy's move. She didn't know whether to take the dare or not. Looking around, she didn't see anyone coming. She noticed that Jake was still swimming. She unbelted her shorts, in a quick move she took her halter off and ran for the water. It was great, swimming without a suit was swift and without effort. Jake swam back to the beach and was now climbing out. When Joy reached the beach she grabbed her clothes and ran to some bushes to dress.

"How did you like the swim?"

"It was great. I didn't realize that swimming in the nude was so free."

The feeling between them was gone, they both realized it at the same time. Slowly they started back to the car. It was a silent ride back to Joy's. Both were deep in thought. Joy wondered why Jake was so bashful, why he didn't take the opportunity to go as far as possible. Jake was thinking what a dummy he was. He felt that Joy was his for the asking, but something in the deep recesses of his mind made it impossible for him to make love to Joy. She was so desireable, so beautiful, the more he thought about it the madder he got at himself.

Joy could see that something was bothering him. "What's the matter, Jake?"

"Nothing. I was just thinking."

"You're sure?"

"Sure"

As they drove along the bumpy, country road, Jake couldn't shake his mood, he felt cheated and dumb.

Joy moved over closer to him. "Don't worry, Jake, everything will work out."

That night he didn't dream about snakes, he dreamed about Joy. He could see her running in the sand, her hair blowing in the wind. She would turn around and laugh, he would almost catch her, but she would always keep distance between them. He twisted and turned; when he awoke he found the sheet was twisted around his neck.

There didn't seem to be any rest for Jake that night. He dozed, but before long his mother was calling him for breakfast. He dressed slowly, it had seemed like such a short night he wished he could go to bed again.

When he made his appearance, both of his parents looked at him; they didn't say anything, but they did look at each other with a blank stare.

"Good morning, Jake."

"Good morning." He did his best to be cheerful, but there really wasn't much to cheer about.

The day's work was usually outlined at the breakfast table. "Jake, I'd like for you to put the cattle in the north pasture today, the grass is green on that pasture. I've hired Fred George to help you because I have to attend a meeting in Parsons today. I'll see you tonight."

Jake went to the pasture with a heavy heart. Fred George would have a few stories to tell and that would help a little.

"What happened last night, Fred?" Jake wanted to get the stories started so that he would not have to talk. He had heard Fred talk about having a hangover. Jake had never had one because he didn't drink, but today he felt like he had a giant hangover.

The day's work helped some. The cattle were hot and thirsty, they were also hungry. The summer heat and the lack of rain had driven the cattle into a frenzy. They darted and hooked at each other, they bawled and snorted. Jake and Fred didn't push them, they had all day to do the job.

About noon Jake was riding point, he waved to Fred to slow the herd down, it was time to eat. Both had a balogna sandwich in their saddlebags. The water from their canteens was hot, but it was wet. Jake wished that he had some jerki, it would be sweet and tasty.

Jake was counting the days, there were so many things that he wanted to do. He wondered why he hadn't heard from Beverly this week. When he rode back home he put up his horse, fed him, saw that there was plenty of extra water. Walking toward the house he noticed his mother waiting on the porch.

"A long distance phone call came for you this afternoon."

"Who from?"

"It was Beverly's mother."

"What did she say?"

"She said that Beverly was in a car accident and is in the hospital."

"Where?"

"I believe she said at the Public Health Service Hospital in Lawton, Oklahoma."

"Was she seriously injured?"

"No, she said to tell you that she was bruised, and her right leg received a fracture. She will have to wear a cast for six weeks."

It all came so fast that he simply sat down on the porch and looked out in space. Finally he stood up. He knew what he had to do, he had to see Beverly.

"Where is Dad? I need to talk to him."

"He went to town, he'll be home any time."

"I'm going to get my things together, then I'm going to town to get my car serviced."

Jake went to his room and started packing. He hardly knew what he was doing, he felt like a robot.

His mother came into the room and said, "Jake, let me do your packing while you go ahead and get your car serviced."

"OK, Mother, thanks."

It almost never rains in Kansas in August, but large thunderheads covered the sky. Cool currents coming down from Colorado had mixed with the warm gulf current from the south and the entire countryside was engulfed in a summer rainstorm.

Jake hadn't noticed that his bug was almost out of gas. It stopped when he was about halfway to town. He was already upset, and this was the last straw. There was only one thing to do, start walking. He locked his car and strode off as fast as he could. He hadn't gone far when he heard a car approaching, so he stopped and held out his thumb. It turned out to be Joy. He really hadn't thought of calling Joy before he left, he hadn't thought much about anything except Beverly.

"You picked a bad day to have car trouble."

"Yes, I ran out of gas. I have to go to a hospital in Lawton to see Beverly. I got a call from her mother that she was injured in a car accident."

"I seem to be your luck today."

"You sure are, and have been for a long time."

"This is the devil's day." Joy didn't know why she said it, but she did. "Do you think enough of Beverly to marry her?"

Jake was on the spot, she had called his hand. "I really don't know."

"You don't?"

Everyone was on his back today. As the car bounced along he didn't say anything, he was deep in thought.

"Hey, we are almost there. Where do you buy your gasoline?"

"It doesn't matter. The first place that you see will be fine."

"Do you want me to take you back to your car?"

"'No, I'll get the service man to take me back."

Joy pulled in at the first service station she came to. Jake crawled out and said earnestly, "On the level, I don't know, but when I make up my mind everyone will know."

The rain had let up a little. The man at the service station loaned him a can, and one of the helpers took him back to his car. This time the rain really came down.

"Damn, I sure won't get started tonight."

"Where is it you're going?"

"Oh, my girl in Oklahoma was hurt in a car wreck, and I hoped to get started tonight. I have to get my car serviced, and with this rain...I don't know."

"Better wait until tomorrow, kinda bad out now."

"Yeah, I think I will."

Jake got his car serviced then drove home as fast as possible. His father and mother were in the kitchen drinking coffee, he could see them through the window. Parking the bug in a vacant shed, he ran into the house.

His father said, "We were just talking about Beverly's accident. Sit down, your mother will have supper ready in a few minutes. Jake and his father moved over to two large chairs while his mother went about the business of putting their supper on the table.

Jake's father was the first to speak, "I know it isn't exactly my business, however, Indian elders have long been searched out for their thoughts. If you want them I will speak, otherwise it will be your decision."

"Yes, Dad, I would appreciate your judgment."

"I know you care for two girls. This is not unusual for a young man, and some older men sometimes do the same thing. You seem to care more for Beverly, perhaps because she is Indian, perhaps not. What are you going to tell Joy? You know she cares

123

for you."

"Yes, Dad, I know. I guess I wasn't going to tell her anything. It bothers me, because I do like Joy, I like her a lot. If it were not for Beverly, it would be Joy. I never really promised her anything, but I care for her a lot."

"Young women are usually looking for husbands, this is the marriageable age. They seldom want to be good friends." Jake's father continued slowly, "I know it will be hard, it is always hard to be a man, but I think you should tell Joy that Beverly is the girl you intend to marry."

While they ate their supper, they made an attempt at small talk but it fell flat.

When he stood up from the table Jake said, "I'm going over to Joy's, I need to talk to her." His parents didn't say anything, they just looked at each other.

Mrs. Hollman answered the door. "Come on in, Jake. Joy is dressing, she'll be out in a minute. How are your folks?"

"They're fine."

"And you?"

"I'm sure it's just like your place, there is always something to do on a farm."

"Yes, there is always something to do." Then she said, sympathetically, "I'm sure sorry to hear about your friend in Oklahoma. Joy was telling me she was in a wreck." Mrs. Hollman had been careful not to say, "girlfriend," but Jake knew what she was thinking.

"Yes, it was too bad." That's as far as he got because Joy came into the room.

"Hi, Jake, it's nice to see you, rain and all."

Jake stalled as long as he could. "I have something to tell you."

Mrs. Hollman could see that they wanted to be alone, so she went into the other room. They sat in chairs across from each other as if they were strangers.

"I told you earlier today that I would let you know about Beverly when I made up my mind." Joy flinched, her entire body reacted. "I'm going to ask Beverly to marry me." Joy started to say something, but she couldn't speak. "You are real special to me, I guess it is just one of those things."

Deep down Joy had felt this was going to happen, but she

124

had prayed that it wouldn't. Her head bowed a little, tears ran down her face.

"I'm glad to hear it from you, Jake. At least you are man enough to tell me." Still composed, but obviously shaken she continued, "I wish you the best of everything." She went over and kissed him quickly, then left the room.

It was over. He felt like a son of a bitch. Going home. he recalled Joy's reaction. She looked beaten, and she was the last person in the world he would want to hurt.

7

Joseph Rainwater had been in Viet Nam a long time, too long really. He vounteered for the hard jobs, this to prove how tough he was, he wanted everyone to know he was a man. Now he was tired of the killing, the heat, the long periods of waiting. He felt exhausted. During his last Rest and Relaxation leave he had spent the entire time with a pickup. She said she was Hawaiian, and she might have been, because she looked like she was a combination of several ethnic groups. She was really stacked, and she gave him his money's worth. As good as she had been, she didn't excite him. All of the girls over here were after a quick buck. They would smile, drink their drink, and smile again. It had been exciting when he first came over, but now he wanted to go home, to eat some Indian camp stew. He wanted to be around his people, this was what he missed most of all.

Joseph took out his little black book, it was dog-eared, a lot of the names had been crossed out. Most of the girls had married, a lot of them he didn't remember, it seemed so long ago. He kept turning the pages, the L's, the N's, the P's. He saw the name Ross, Beverly. That's the one, she was the girl that he left behind. He wondered about her, it was so long ago. "Well," he told himself, "there is one way to find out, and that is to write." Joseph wasn't much of a letter writer, but he was inspired. He poured out his heart and soul, painting a picture of devotion and thoughtfulness.

When Beverly received the letter she was surprised, she read it over again. It had been such a long time since she had heard from Joseph. She remembered their good-byes, how they had promised each other that they would write every day, and they did for awhile. But as the weeks and years passed by, fewer and fewer letters were mailed. This was the first time she had heard from Joseph in eight months.

"Mother, guess who I heard from today."

"Probably Jake, you hear from him almost everyday."

"No, this letter is from Joseph Rainwater. You remember him, I used to see a lot of him before he went to Viet Nam. I sort of liked him, I wonder what he is like now."

Her mother was quick to pick this up, "The war ruins most of the young men, they come home with a taste for drinking and running around. It takes a long time to get Viet Nam out of their systems."

"He says he is coming home, and the first place he is coming is here. You remember his home is in Mountain View. He belongs to the corn clan, they'll probably have a big celebration for him, they always do." Beverly was wondering if his letter was written just to get her won over to his way of thinking. She suspected it was.

Joseph had already served his time in Viet Nam and was just awaiting transportation. It was a forty hour flight to the States, and here he was in Camp Pendleton. This was where he took his boot training. He wondered what happened to the men he had trained with. The camp looked unreal. It was so different from the one he had just left. He wondered if the recruits knew what they were in for.

During the processing he was encouraged not to talk to the recruits, and he knew why. They all believed that they would come back, actually very few of them would see the States again. The recruits usually believed the war movies they had seen, each thought of himself as a hero. He could hear a sergeant making negative comments about civilian life, and offering the lure of a big check to re-enlist, but he was ready for a change. He got his discharge, back pay, and transportation home.

His plane was on time to Oklahoma City, then he caught a bus and went to the downtown station. It was full of old men and mothers with children. They all looked tired, it depressed him. He wanted to be on his way, but he still had an hour to wait for his bus. A beer would taste good.

"Hey, buddy, where can I get a bottle of beer?"

"Right down the street"

The beer joint wasn't hard to find, he could hear the music coming out of the open door. The crowd looked jovial, and he could tell that most of them had been bending their arm for some time. A girl stepped in front of him, "I can show you a good time, soldier." She was unsteady on her feet. This was the thing he was tired of, but he still wanted a bottle of beer, so he walked past her, not saying anything. He sat down on a bar stool and ordered a Budweiser. After a few swallows he began to relax, the noise didn't bother him, and the drunks left him alone. They seemed to sense that he wanted to be alone, some of them had been hit and knocked across the room for less. One bottle satisfied him. He walked out of the beer joint and back to the statin.

His bus was on the ramp, so he climbed aboard and flopped down in a seat. Before long he fell asleep. When he awoke the bus had stopped and all the passengers were getting out. He looked at the sign over the door of the station, "Carnegie, Oklahoma." He knew that he would soon be home. Now he was restless and time seemed to drag. He looked out of the window of the bus, trying to see some familiar landscape, but is was too dark. When the bus finally arrived at Mountain View he got off, claimed his baggage, and walked to an all night cafe. He recognized Freddy Whiteowl. He looked sleepy, like he wasn't used to staying up late at night.

"Hi, Freddy"

Freddy looked around, blinked several times, then finally recognized Joseph.

"Where have you been? I haven't seen you in a long time."

"I've been in Viet Nam."

"Oh, I thought you were at Fort Sill."

This made Joseph mad, but he didn't say anything as he realized that Freddy wasn't all there. He felt tired and cross, all he wanted now was to hit the sack. He had been on the road for about sixty hours without much rest. This was home, sweet home. It was like Christmas and all of the holidays wrapped up in one. But this wasn't the night for celebration. He realized that he was so tired he could hardly stand, his ears were ringing from the change in altitude. He was stiff and sore from bouncing around in different types of transportation. The hamburger and coffee gave him a lift, so he had another.

He needed a ride home, it was eight miles out in the country. "Freddy, how about taking me home?"

"How much will you give me."

"I'll buy your gasoline."

"I would rather have the money, besides, you can't buy gasoline this time of night. I'll take you for five bucks."

Joseph thought it over, he hated to part with the five bucks, but he hated to think of walking the eight miles.

"Would you cut it down for a GI?"

"Same charge to all, they don't give me a discount on my gasoline."

"OK, you're on. Let's go."

Freddy had an old Chevrolet that looked like it was on its last legs. Joseph didn't care, just as long as it would get him home. Freddy knew all of the car's weaknesses, he nursed it along, watching the road ahead for stray cattle. They pulled up in front of the square, frame house. It had been white when it was built, but now the years had taken their toll. The dogs started barking, Joseph called them by name. At first they didn't respond, then they seemed to remember and came up to him wagging their tails, and prancing around. Suddenly he saw a light in the house, he could see the outline of his mother and father. He gave Freddy a five dollar bill, grabbed his bags and ran to his mother's side. She placed her arms around him and gave him a big hug, his father reached out and grasped his hand, then put an arm around his shoulder. Nothing was said, he was home.

They went into the house, it looked like yesterday, calendars on the wall, pictures of the family on the desk in the corner. It warmed his heart.

"Do you want anything to eat?"

"No, I had something to eat in town. Where are all of the kids?"

"They're all asleep, but they're not kids any longer, they're in junior and senior high school."

Joseph thought, "Have I been away that long?"

The house had a small stairway to the second story. When they built the house it was unfinished, and Joseph had completed it because he wanted a place for himself. He took all of his gear

129

up the stairs with him, and his mother and father followed him. "Your bed is all made, son. We thought you might be coming home soon."

"But how did you know?"

"We didn't, really, but I had a dream the other night. It was so real that the next day I cleaned your room and made up your bed. Your father said I was putting too much faith in a dream."

His father said, "Go on to bed, son, we know you are tired. We'll talk to you in the morning."

Joseph didn't need any prodding, it was very late, in fact it was almost morning. He took off his clothes, jumped in bed, and was asleep almost as fast as he hit the bed. He slept late, his mother kept the rest of the family quiet.

When he came downstairs it was almost noon. His brothers and sisters were waiting, they felt a little awkward. But his mother said, "Come, this is your brother, give him an Indian welcome." This broke the ice and they came forward, shaking hands, putting their arms around his waist, looking at him in wonder.

His mother had fixed stacks of hot cakes, along with eggs and coffee. The family was hungry but they had waited. Eating together had given them a relaxed and happy feeling.

His little brother, Al, was the first to ask a question. "Are you glad to be home, Joseph?" Everybody laughed.

"Why do you think I wouldn't be glad to be home?"

"Well, you are a soldier and I thought you would be fighting." They laughted again.

"That's true, Al, but I'm no longer in the Marines, I'm a civilian."

"What's a civilian?"

"That's someone who is not in the armed forces."

"The armed forces, what's that? I thought you were in the Marines."

"The Marines is a part of the armed forces, like the Army and the Navy."

"I don't understand."

"Don't worry about it, you will understand soon enough."

The family became quiet. They were proud of Joseph. There were many Indian families that had lost sons in the Viet Nam conflict. They had some misgivings about this war that never ended, it had been going on as long as some of the children could remember. They also knew that some of the young men came back exhausted. They wouldn't talk about the war, they drank too much and seemed restless. They felt that some of the young men were witched, so they had all-night sings for them and give-aways. But still the men remained deep within themselves. It was like a sickness, and they hoped that Joseph didn't have it. They wanted to hear him laugh, to sing, to be happy. They would have to wait to see how the war had affected him.

It seemed to Joseph that each member of his family was watching him. They had all changed. His mother and father looked more familiar than his sisters and brothers. He thought that, with the passage of time, he would be able to feel a part of the family again. They had opened their hearts to him, but he was not completely at ease with them.

"What happened to the old gang that I used to run around with?"

His mother filled him in on all of the marriages, deaths, those who had gone on to school and those who had dropped out. He finally got around to asking about Beverly.

"She is going to the University of Oklahoma this fall. She is a beautiful young woman." His mother was direct. "Are you thinking about her?" This wasn't exactly what he meant, but everybody got the idea.

Joseph's face was flushed, "Yes, I would like to see her, it has been a long time."

"I wouldn't get too excited about seeing her, I hear that she met a man from Kansas at the American Indian Exposition, and is engaged to him."

"But she can't do that."

"Why not?"

"Because she said that she would wait for me."

"You were gone so long I guess she became lonesome."

Joseph could feel the back of his neck burning, it always did this when he got mad.

His mother could tell that he was upset. "Beverly is a young, attractive woman at the marriageable age. Did you write to her often? And did you also plan ot wait for her?"

His mother was right, and he didn't want to argue with her.

"If you're interested in her, why don't you go over and see her? I saw her in the store yesterday, I know that she is home."

"That's a good idea."

The rest of the family smiled. His father hadn't said anything.

"What do you think, Papa?"

"Well, son, I think too many years have slipped by, but you never can tell. The best way is to go over and find out for yourself."

His parents seemed so old and solid, they had been like that as long as he could remember. They never argued, at least not in front of the children. They seemed to work together, this was their way of life. He also knew they would like to see him settle down. The thought hung in his mind.

Joseph could see why Beverly had become interested in someone else, but still, she had promised. However, he knew he had not kept his promise. He had had many girls of all races, how could he expect Beverly to remain true to him? The sand seemed to be running out, but he was going to see her anyway. This had all been going through his mind while he was having breakfast.

As soon as everyone was through eating, he excused himself and went to his room to dress. Civilian clothes felt so funny, they were so light, the shoes felt like he was barefooted.

His father loaned him his car. As he approached Beverly's house he thought about the Ross family. Beverly and her mother lived here alone, the rest of the family had long since departed. Beverly's mother had a herd of cattle, she hired two men to do most of the ranching. Mrs. Ross had a way of making money and hanging on to it. A lot of her Indian neighbors felt that she didn't see any reason to be poor, or to give away her cattle to those who wouldn't work. Indians are the world's best critics, they tried to find fault with her, but she knew that they envied her. Every Christmas she had a big dinner and gave out presents, Indian style. This kept the peace. Secretly they admired her, but outwardly they continued to say mean things about the Ross family. Joseph didn't know if he could measure up to what Mrs. Ross wanted in a son-in-law. He was rather slow in knocking at the door.

"Hello, Mrs. Ross."

"Hello, Joseph, it's nice to see you home again. I know your mother and father were glad to see you and to have you back from Viet Nam. So many of our boys were killed and, even worse, some came home with the sickness."

Joseph knew what she was talking about, it was like a plague.

"Is Beverly home?"

"Please come in, she will be out in a minute."

Joseph found a chair in a corner of the room. This home wasn't like most Indian homes, no calendars, no cloth thrown over the sofa and chairs, few pictures. The furniture was well kept and the room had wall-to-wall carpet. He felt ill at ease.

When Beverly came out he saw that she was much taller and had filled out. She was indeed a young woman, and not the thin girl he had left.

"Come on in the kitchen and let's have a cup of coffee, we can talk." She was completely at ease. She set two cups and saucers out, and went to the stove to get the coffee pot.

Joseph notice the difference in this kitchen and the one at home. It was such a pleasant place, orderly, well kept.

Joseph knew that he had a long way to go, perhaps if he got Beverly away from here he would have a better chance.

"How about going walking down by your pond, you remember, where we used to go fishing."

"Alright. Mother, we are going down to the pond for awhile."

The day was beautiful, everything sparkled. Joseph had been around the sounds of gunfire for so long that it seemed strangely quiet. They found their favorite spot, it was grassy and shaded. An old cottonwood tree had fallen years ago and made an ideal spot to sit. Joseph actually didn't know where to start, so he just looked at Beverly.

"Why are you looking at me like that?"

"Because I haven't seen you in such a long time. I wanted to bring you into my being once more."

"What do you mean?"

"When we parted we promised we would wait for each other."

"Yea, and we did at first, then you quit writing and I didn't know what had happened to you. I thought about you a lot at first, and missed you so very much. It wasn't easy. I asked mother about it, and she said to get busy, that time would pass and it would heal the hurt in my heart." They were both lost in thought for awhile, then Beverly continued. "I thought I could wait for you the rest of my life, but I was wrong. I was so lonely, I thought about you day and night. I spent a lot of time writing to you, and I did hear from you at first. As you know, I hadn't heard from you in a long time."

"Is there any way I can make it up to you?"

"We can think about the past but we can't make it up. Once

a day is gone, it is gone forever. Our past is gone forever, it was a young interlude."

Joseph didn't say a word for a few minutes. He had been completely stopped.

"It was the war. I would have written to you more often if I had had the time. Sometimes out lives were not worth a dime. We lived on hope, it was just enough to keep us alive. We were constantly on the move."

"Didn't you ever get any R and R?"

"Yes, I did and it passed so fast."

"You could have written then."

"I guess I was selfish and didn't think of anyone but myself."

"I didn't go with any boys for over a year after you left. Mother said I couldn't live like that. She encouraged me to see other young men, she said it wasn't natural to be alone so much. I still like you, Joseph, but I should tell you that I have become engaged to another young man."

"Who is he, do I know him?"

"He used to live at Hog Creek Mission near Anadarko, now he lives in Kansas. I met him this summer, sort of a spur of the moment thing. He's coming here soon to pay his respects to the family."

Joseph really wasn't ready for this. he thought it would be cold turkey, all he would have to do was arrive and say, "Here I am!"

He tried another tactic. "If we could go out together, we probably could pick up where we left off, how about going someplace tonight?" Beverly didn't want to hurt him since he had meant something to her at one time. Jake would understand, but she didn't know about her mother.

"I want to think it over, let's go up to the house and get something to drink."

Joseph thought he had a foot in the door. They walked hand in hand up to the house, talking about the gossip around mountain View. Beverly brought him up-to-date on the happenings of the gang of kids that they both knew. Joseph opened the door for Beverly when they reached the house. She went immediately to the refrigerator and brought out two bottles of pop. She motioned him over to a chair on the other side of the table. It was deliberate, the further away she stayed from him the better.

When her mother came in Beverly asked, "Mother, can I go out with Joseph tonight?"

Her mother was not reluctant to speak, "What about Jake, do you think he would like it?"

"This really isn't a date, we just want to visit old friends and talk about old times. I won't stay out late."

Beverly's mother didn't have any doubts about her daughter, she knew she had a good head on her, but she also knew Joseph. He had been away for a long time, and had picked up ideas from foreign lands. She knew the ways of soldiers, she had seen them come up from Fort Sill during World War I and II. They were looking for the same thing, young girls and women who were willing.

Actually, Beverly felt excited about going with Joseph, she was anxious to hear about his travels. She didn't have any illusions about him. He had been to Viet Nam and she knew that he had known foreign women. This didn't bother her, because she assumed most men had known other women before they married.

Joseph called for her at seven o'clock and they drove to Mountain View. He remembered a favorite drive-in and thought it wouldbe a good place to break the ice.

Beverly asked, "What do you plan to do now that you are home?"

"To tell you the truth, you are one of the main reasons I hit for home after I was released. I thought we could take up where we left off."

This upset Beverly, she had hoped that he wouldn't bring it up. "Tell me about your travels, I would like to hear all about the places where you have been."

"Viet Nam was hot, and a lot of the time it rained, making it miserable. When we were not in combat it wasn't so bad. We had tents, and in some places there were actually barracks. There were times when we didn't have anything to do but drink beer and watch movies. I went to Saigon one time, but most of the time it was off limits. It was just like any other town; a lot of dance halls, beer joints, and just about any kind of entertainment you want, if you want to pay for it."

"Did you take advantage of any of it?" Beverly was teasing him now.

"What do you mean?"

"You know what I mean. I read about the bar girls in some

135

magazines."

"Oh, there were girls all right, but none like you. That's one of the reasons I wanted to leave."

"And what were the other reasons?"

Joseph hesitated a moment. "I guess that really is the big reason, the others are to sleep in a house, get a job, and settle down."

"Sounds interesting. Do you think you can settle down after being on the move for so long?"

Joseph was quick to answer that question, "Yes, I'm ready!"

"Were the bar girls interesting? Were they nice?"

"I don't know if they were nice or not."

"Why not?"

"Because they couldn't speak English."

"You mean all you did was to look at each other?"

This line of conversation was getting on Joseph's nerves, it wasn't any of her business what he did with his R and R. He wondered if Beverly was asking these questions on purpose. It was probably a way of testing him.

"I'm sorry if I brought up unpleasant memories."

"I was just thinking."

"Yes, I know."

It was then that Joseph realized how much Beverly had changed. When he left she was still in high school, and they were so much in love. Now she was different, more like her mother, always in command. He turned and looked at her closely, she was lovely, truly beautiful. How could a girl with such beauty be such a brain. Most girls were flattered by his attention. Could this be the reason he was attracted to her, he wanted something that he couldn't get? What should he try next?

"How about a show?"

"There's no theatre in Mountain View, the last one closed last summer."

"Well, then we can drive to Hobart, it isn't far and I need a change."

"That would be fun."

Joseph was surprised, he thought Beverly would have some excuse for not wanting to go.

The car windows were rolled down and they enjoyed feeling the rushing wind. But the wind and the motor noise made it impossible to talk, especially since Beverly sat close to the door. "Why don't you move over here? Then we could talk."

At first she acted as if she didn't hear, then she moved over a little closer. "What shall we talk about?"

"What about you? What do you plan to do after you have finished college?"

"I'm majoring in sociology, and I hope to work with Indians. Eventually I would like to teach in college."

This stopped Joseph cold, he knew that Beverly was smart, but he didn't realize that there was such a difference between them.

They reached the main part of Hobart and parked within a block of the Ritz theatre. Joseph got out and started down the sidewalk when he realized Beverly was still sitting in the car. "We are here."

"Yes, I know." She still didn't move. "I'm waiting for you to open the door."

Joseph walked over and opened the door. Beverly stepped out and gave him her pixie smile. He was mad, he didn't like her kind of jokes. She had tried to show him up, to make a fool out of him.

They walked up to the window and Joseph bought two tickets. They hadn't even looked to see what the name of the show was, it really didn't make any difference. They sat there in the darkness, scarcely moving. After they had been in the theatre a while it didn't seem so dark. At first they had hardly paid any attention to the movie, it turned out to be a story of the army in Viet Nam. This was all he needed. The bar girls were played up big, with the GIs as suckers. Joseph managed a weak smile, he mumbled to himself.

Beverly whispered, 'What did you say?"

"They are showing just one side of the war."

People in the theatre turned around to stare. Joseph felt mad and foolish. After awhile the movie showed the actual fighting. He reached over and took Beverly's hand in his. She responded with a quick glance, he could tell that it didn't mean anything to her. Joseph felt dejected. He got up, went to the foyer and bought some popcorn. He slipped back into his seat, handed Beverly her sack and sat glumly eating. After he had finished, he reached over and took her hand in his. It was like a sandpaper hand with all of the salt on it. After more shooting the movie came to a grinding end, the hero left for home and the bar girl was left to her own devices

As they drove home, the air was full of night insects that tried to come in the car. They raised the windows, but it made it too hot. Soon the windshield was covered, it made it difficult to see. They stopped for a minute and Joseph tried to scrape off some of the bugs. They swarmed around him. Seeing that he was about to be covered, he shouted, "Start the car."
Beverly moved into the driver's seat and started slowly down the road, sticking her head out of the window. The insects soon covered her, she stopped and Joseph ran around the car and got in the driver's seat. He couldn't see, but he was driving as fast as he could. Soon they started going uphill, and the insects disappeared as if by magic. They could see a farmhouse down the road, so Joseph drove in and knocked on the door.

A friendly voice called out, "Come on in."

"No, we just need some water to wash off our windshield."

A man brought out a tin bucket and dropped it into the well, and then hauled it up by pulling the rope. "Here you are. What happened, did you loose the water in your car?"

"No, we ran into a swarm of bugs, they completely covered our windshield, we couldn't see.

It suddenly dawned on Joseph that he could take advantage of this situation. While Beverly and the man talked, he raised the hood of the car and pulled the wire out of the timer, not all the way, just enough to keep the car from making electical contact. They stood around talking for awhile, said their good-byes and got into the car to return home. When Joseph put the key in the switch the car wouldn't start, he got out and pretended to work on it.

"What's wrong?"

"I don't know, I guess we'll have to spend the night here."

"Can't that man help you get it started? Maybe we could push it."

Joseph got out and talked to the man. Soon he brought a pickup out and they hooked on. The pickup was just about shot, and couldn't gey up enough powere to pull the car. This turn of events upset Beverly. She call to Joseph, "What are we going to do? Perhaps you could borrow his pickup. I can't spend the night here, what would people think? Do you think these people have a telephone?"

"No."

"Maybe we could get out on the road and catch a ride." She started walking over to the road. Joseph didn't want this to happen, a car might accidentally come by and his plan would be spoiled.

"I don't think any cars will be coming by this time of night."

"Maybe not, but I'm going to stand here and wait. I've just got to get home tonight."

Joseph felt like a fool standing there on the road, but he didnl't have any choice. He tried to think of something to say. He started a conversation, it was short-lived. He could see the headlights of a car in the distance. The countryside was fog covered. The headlights bounced around crazily. From the sounds it made it must be an older model car. Beverly inched her way into the road with Joseph close behind her.

Beverly took off her jacket and began to wave. She was out in the middle of the road, but Joseph reached and pulled her back. "What are you trying to do, get yourself killed?"

"No, I'm trying to catch a ride."

Sure enough, the car came to a grinding stop. "What's the matter, your car break down?"

"Yes, we're trying to catch a ride, our car won't start."

"How far are you going? Say, don't I know you, aren't you Beverly Ross?"

"Yes, I am, who are you?"

"I'm Joe Whiteowl, Freddy's younger brother. I've seen you around Mountain View, I guess you don't remember me."

"Are you going home? We would like to catch a ride back to Mountain View."

"Yes, I'm on my way home."

Joseph stepped out of the shadows, he wasn't in the mood for small talk. "I'm with Beverly."

"What's wrong with your car?"

"We pulled up in this yard to clean the bugs off of our windshield, and the car won't start."

"Do you want me to look at it?"

"No."

"It won't take me but a minute. I'm a good mechanic, and there aren't many cars that I can't start."

This was the last thing that Joseph wanted. All he needed was to have him find out that he had tampered with his own car so it wouldn't start.

But Beverly said, "Go ahead and look at it, Joe. You might be able to get it started."

Joseph was desperate, "I don't want anybody working on my car but me."

Beverly was stopped for only a minute, "Well, then we can ride home with you, Joe. You only live a short distance from me."

"Pile in, you're welcome to the back seat." He nodded his head toward the girl in the front seat with him, "This is Alice Kaulity." She didn't say anything. With a jump and a grinding of gears, they headed for home.

The car lurched and rocked as it bumped along the road. Joseph sat in a corner with his eyes closed, he was mad and he showed it. Beverly didn't do anything to help, as she was mad also. The evening had started out to be a lot of fun, and it was, until now. Joseph's mad gradually began to wear off. He knew he had to make an effort to be friendly or he wouldn't ever see Beverly again.

"Beverly."

"Yes."

"Are you mad at me?"

"I guess I'm mad because the evening turned out the way it did."

"I'll tell you what."

"What?"

"Let's try it again."

Beverly hesitated. "I'll think about it."

"I'll go get my car in the morning, and have it ready to go by tomorrow evening."

"What do you want to do?"

"Let's really turn it on, how about Oklahoma City? I know a good place to dance."

"I didn't know you had been to Oklahoma City since you came back home."

"I haven't, but I heard Freddy talking about a good place, he goes over there about every week."

"I don't know, I would rather not go so far, it would be very late when we got home. I would rather stay at home, especially after tonight. I'm afraid mother would take a dim view of it."

Joseph was ready to do anything to stay in her good graces, so he didn't push the point.

Joe Whiteowl wasn't as talkative as his brother, besides, he was more interested in Alice Kaulity than in talking to the occupants in the back seat. There wasn't much conversation during the remainder of the ride.

Joseph did manage to slide over toward Beverly. He wanted to put his arm around her, but he was afraid to. His mind wandered back to the girls in Viet Nam, they would do anything for money, at least the ones he knew. He also remembered that he was tired of them, and that he wanted a girl he could depend on. Beverly was such a girl.

They drove up to Beverly's house, and Joseph walked her to the door.

"Good night Joseph. Everything started out alright, but I guess circumstances, or fate, had something to do with what happend." She reached out her hand for a handshake. Joseph was pleased that she made such a concession.

Joseph walked back to the waiting car.

"Did you give her a good night kiss?"

"No. She didn't seem interested."

"Boy, you are sure some lover."

"I thought I was, but I have a lot to learn about women. These girls back home are a lot different than the ones overseas."

Joe took Joseph home. "Hey, wait a minute, I want to pay for your gas for bringing us home."

"I don't know what we would have done without you." Joseph would soon have himself believing it.

Joseph went to bed, but he didn't sleep, he was wondering how he could win Beverly over. Actually, he was surprised that she would go with him considering the fact that she was engaged to the man from Kansas.

It had taken Joseph all day to get his car home. He hurried through supper, explaining to his mother that he was going over to Beverly's.

"Don't you know that Beverly is already spoken for? Besides she is practically one of your kinfolks.

"Oh, Mother, I don't go for all that Indian style kinfolks stuff, actually we are not related, as you well know."

"But all of the folks around here consider you two related, and that's what counts." She looked at the calendar and wondered when Beverly would be going to school. She mumbled to herself.

and shook her head. Joseph should marry out of his clan, and he should bring his wife home, that way they could teach her the ways of the home.

Joseph had spent the night tossing and turning, but his plans wouldn't jell. He had to do something that would cause Beverly to change her mind, something that would make her obligated to him. He thought about the girls in Viet Nam, he could take her out and get her drunk, and spend the night with her. However, this wasn't very likely and he knew it. He might get drunk and see what happened.

Beverly felt she had seen enough of Joseph, but when he showed up the next evening, she invited him in.

"I wanted ot see you and tell you how sorry I am everything developed the way it did."

"Forget it, it wasn't your fault. Come on in the kitchen I have some cokes in the refrigerator."

Joseph was glad she was so friendly, and that she didn't know what he had been thinking. They sat there for awhile, not saying much. Finally Joseph said, "Let's go down to the drive-in, we will probably run into some kids we know."

Joseph certainly had not planned it this way, but suddenly he said, "I've been thinking, we are of the same tribe, and know each other well, why don't we get married?"

Beverly was so startled she didn't know what to say. Slowly the words came out, "Joseph, you know that I am engaged, I consider you a good friend but nothing more."

Joseph felt completely confused, he couldn't think of why he had asked her in the first place. Now that she had turned him down he was mad. He reached over, turned on the ignition, and started the car. Driving out of the drive-in without picking up thier order, he blazed full speed ahead down a country road. Beverly was yelling for him to stop, he heard her but didn't pay any attention. He was in Viet Nam, the "gookes" were after him, he had a smile on his face. The sound was not of bullets, but the siren of the police car. Although Joseph knew the country roads, in his excitement he forgot that most of the corners are square, and when he came to a corner he didn't make it.

When he awoke, there was a nurse standing near. "Where am I?"

"You're in a hospital."

"Which one?"

"The Public Health Hospital in Lawton, Oklahoma."

"What happened?"

"You were in a wreck."

This seemed to satisfy Joseph for awhile. The only thing he could recall was Viet Nam. He wondered if it could be a grenade or a land mine that he had tangled with. Other men had been mutilated, their hands and legs blown off. Their screams were in his mind. Once in a while a nurse would come in and give him some medication. He tried to think of a sensible question, but couldn't manage it. Why was a beautiful girl in his dreams, who could she be? She appeared to be familiar in some ways, but he could not remember where he had known her. Finally he slept. but in his dream there were images that he didn't understand, he cried out.

When he opened his eyes a nurse said, "You were screaming, so I came down to see what was the matter."

"What is the matter?"

"That's what I came to find out."

Joseph tried to think, he wondered why he couldn't put things together. About the time he started to make sense out of his being here, he felt himself slipping away.

When his mother came in that afternoon, he had a lot of questions to ask her. "Tell me, Mother, what happened?"

"I can only tell you a few things, you will have to fill in the rest. You and Beverly left her house, then went to the drive-in, from there no one seems to know what happened. Several people said they saw you racing out of town with the highway patrol after you."

He remembered this, but it didn't make any sense. His mother didn't say anything for a long time, then she asked, "Were you and Beverly drinking?"

"I don't know."

"What do you mean, you don't know?"

"Just what I said, I don't remember."

"Beverly's mother is plenty upset over this."

"What about Beverly?"

"I guess you know she's in this hospital too, her mlother said she will be released soon."

"I would like to see her, do you suppose she would come in and talk? Would you ask her?"

Mrs. Rainwater was thoughtful, "I really don't know, I feel mixed up."

There was a knock on the door, Joseph's mother went to the

143

door and opened it. It was Beverly's mother. Joseph's mother offered her hand, and Mrs. Ross accepted it. The handclasp was Indian, just a delicate touch, there were no hostile words. If there was anger, it was hidden deep within Mrs. Ross. She was self-possessed, she wanted the upper hand. She walked over to Joseph's bed. "How are you Joseph?" There was no sign of emotion.

"I guess I'm alright. I was just trying to figure out what happened."

"You don't know?"

"No."

"Were you and Beverly drinking?"

"No, but beyond that I just don't remember."

Mrs. Ross looked directly at Joseph. Slowly and without malice, with words so soft and well chosen she said, "You know Beverly is engaged to a man in Kansas named, Jake. I plan to give him my blessing when he comes. I have called him, and I think he will be here soon. There will be a feast. First I must conlsult Beverly's old grandfather to see if the match is right. He has the power to see if the marriage will work. He will have to talk to Jake and ask him some questions." She reached out her hand to Joseph, he took it. That was all, she left the room as quietly as she had entered. It was a real Indian meeting, nobody had lost face.

8

Jake was packed and ready to go to Oklahoma to see Beverly. "Dad, there is something I need to talk to you about before I leave."

"Alright, let's go out on the on the porch."

"I plan to ask Beverly to marry me."

"I thought you would."

"There is something that I don't quite understand."

"What is it?"

"Beverly's mother said she wanted to know how I would support Beverly. She also said somethig about gifts of horses and cattle.

His father had a pleasant smile on his face, "Yes, the western Indian tribes always exchange gifts. In the old days the bridegroom always had to furnish horses for the brides parents."

"How come?"

"Just a custom somebody started. Since then, a marriage among the western tribes has always been a big ceremony. From what you have told me, Mrs. Ross is a pretty sharp mother."

"I don't understand trading horses for a wife, it doesn't seem right."

"It's not a matter of right and wrong, it's just an Indian custom in western Oklahoma. Do you want to marry Beverly?"

"Yes."

"Then you had better follow the customs. You are going to have to give. Really, it's important that the custom be maintained. I'll tell you, let's say five horses and ten cows, and see what Mrs. Ross says. We have plenty."

"Another thing she wanted to know is how I am going to support Beverly. I have about five hundred dollars in the bank."

"Most brides like to say where they are going to live. If you go to college, then you will have to find a place to stay."

"Yes, I know. But with the tuition and all, five hundred dollars isn't much."

"Your mother and I have talked this over, and if Mrs. Ross accepts, let us know, we will drive down and bargain with her. In the old days parents did all of the bargaining, I believe Mrs. Ross is old school."

Jake was relieved, he felt that a big weight had been lifted from his shoulders. "Where will we go in between marriage and school?"

"I would leave that up to Beverly, women usually have ideas about such things."

"I guess I have a lot to learn about marriage and women."

"Yes, I would say that you have a lot to learn."

"Another thing, Mrs. Ross said something about some relative telling whether the marriage was right."

"Another custom."

"And what if he says it isn't?"

"Well, you must remember I know a little about Indians and their customs, I mean, our customs. I'm an Indian too, or had you forgotten?"

"No, I haven't forgotten. I'm also part Indian, and I don't know much except what I learned from you and from Riverside. And I learned a few things this summer in Anadarko."

"Indians love to give and receive gifts."

"But I wouldn't know what to take."

Another grin came across his father's face. "I guess your mother was pretty sure you would soon marry, and that it would be Beverly. Women have a sixth sense about such things. So I had Mr. Crow, down at the general store, send in an order to the Pendleton Company. He was able to get six blankets so I bought all of them. They are real Indian blankets in all colors. They are prized very highly by the western tribes. And I have something special for Beverly. This ring belonged to my sister, and I'm sure she would want you to have it. I think it's beautiful."

146

"Thanks, Dad, I really don't know what to say."

"Oh, that's all right, I think I know how you feel. When you see Beverly tell her that we send our blessings. Oh yes, you'd better ask Beverly about the time and place to give the blankets. She will know about the customs in her tribe. I guess that's all."

They shook hands.

Jake went into the house. His mother was standing near a big box, all smiles. Slowly walking toward Jake, she put her arms around him and held on tight. "Our best to you and Beverly. Oh, shaw, I'm really taking on."

"Thanks, Mom."

"I'll help you put these things in your car."

Jake had a very warm feeling inside as he waved good-bye to his parents. He gunned the motor and was on his way. He was all keyed up, and felt that once he got on the road, he would relax. He had a faint throb in his head, but most of all the fear of the unknown gnawed at him.

There was something about driving that was soothing. Perhaps it was the fact that he was moving. He felt much better now that he was actually doing something, he began to breathe easier. Once you have traveled a road it never seems as long the next time. After he got on the turnpike to Lawton, it didn't take long. He did have some trouble locating the Indian Public Health Service Hospital. He stood outside before going in, wondering what he would say.

He walked slowly into the building and went to the information desk. The girl at the desk said, "Beverly is in room 303, third floor, east. It is in the orthopedic section."

Jake stepped on the elevator, punched number 3, and waited. Like all hospital elevators, this one was large, it was also, slow. The light indicated, 3, and the door opened. He came to a sudden stop, Beverly was sitting in a wheelchair in front of the elevator.

"Hey, Beverly!"

"Jake."

Dropping to his knees, words came tumbling out, both wanted to talk at the same time. "Are you alright? Tell me what happened." People began to stare. Some were waiting to get on the elevator.

"Let's move to the waiting room."

"OK." Jake got behind the wheelchair.

147

"Down that way, it's at the end of the hall."

Fortunately the waiting room was almost empty, one old man sat in a corner, his head bowed.

Jake wheeled Beverly directly in front of his chair. "I was really shook up when your mother called. I could imagine all sorts of terrible things that might have happened to you. Maybe you don't think so, but to me you look great."

Beverly smiled at Jake, "Well, as you can see, my leg is in a cast. the doctor said it was fractured. The cast will have to stay for awhile, other than that, I'm all right. As soon as mother comes for me, I'm going home."

"Is it alright if I go with you?"

"We are expecting you to, we have plenty of room."

Jake eased back in his chair, it was so good to see her.

Beverly inched her wheelchair even closer.Taking Jake's hands in hers, she kissed both of them. Now Jake didn't feel so tired, he reached over to Beverly and kissed her long and hard.

"These days Indian kids don't have any sense of decency," the old man in the corner said, as he got up. Then he walked out.

Beverly said softly, "I love you so much it's hard to hold back, but I think we should wait. The old ones don't understand."

"You're right. There are so many things I want to talk about." Being with her was almost enough, he reached over again and kissed her. He wanted to consume her, she was so appealing. He was like a drunken man, reeling, Beverly intoxicated him.

But the feeling came to an end when he saw Beverly's mother coming down the hall. "I see your mother coming this way."

Beverly backed her wheelchair around, turning it toward her mother. "Hello, Mother."

Her mother didn't say anything, she stooped over and kissed Bevely. She held out her hand to Jake. This time he knew what an Indian handshake should be like, he also knew it was a salutation.

Turning to Beverly she said, "The doctor said you could go home." It was just a flat statement, nothing more. "Jake would you like to go home with us?"

"Yes, I would. I have my volkswagon, I'll follow you."

"I will take Beverly to her room so she can dress, then you can carry her bag."

"I'll wait here, let me know when you are ready."

Beverly wore her familiar blouse and slacks. Her black hair was tied with a small ribbon, making a pony tail. She waved at him as her mother set her bag outside.

"They gave me some crutches, I''ll have to get used to them."

"That won't be hard, I'm sure you have good balance."

Jake wheeled Beverly to the elevator, out on the main floor, and through the main exit. A few patients she had known spoke to her. "Good luck, Beverly. Take care."

Jake wished Beverly could ride with him, but her mother thought Beverly should ride with her. Mrs. Ross was all business, after getting eveything in the car, she backed out and was gone. Jake followed, aware that he was second in command. One of these days he intended to be number one. He was learning, but he still had a long was to go.

Mrs. Ross planned to have her grandfather test Jake. Some people called him a shaman, a medicine man. His name was Ku-ken-ish, although his white teachers had called him Kenneth. He didn't stay in school long as he thought school was a lot of nonsense.

Ku-ken-ish had heard about this Jake, and learned he was not a full blood. He recalled some of the feats that young men were called on to perform, like going up to Rattlesnake Mountain. This was the real test of a man. After much thought he settled on a plan of performance for Jake.

Ku-ken-ish performed several rituals and looked for favorable signs. He talked to the passing south wind to see if it knew anything about this Jake. It promised to ask the north wind. Perhaps it would be better to see what the crow and the coyote knew. Ku-ken-ish had picked up the crow after it was injured by a hunter. The crow had responded to his treatment and regained it's health. Ku-ken-ish would pick berries for the crow. They became good friends. He had also picked up a coyote pup after its mother had been killed by some hunters. Usually coyotes are hard to tame, but this one had responded to the atmosphere of the camp.

Ku-ken-ish still lived on his original allotment of one hundred and sixty acres. He had a summer arbor, a large teepee, and behind it another small, white tent in which he kept his supplies.

When it was hot he moved to the arbor, during the cold winter season he moved back into the teepee. It faced east, this was the direction of life.

The moon and the stars were the guiding light of man's destiny. Ku-ken-ish followed their paths every clear night. He would draw in the sand their relation to each other. From his father he had learned the importance of the wild herbs that grew on his land. He would gather and dry them, to use in his medications. He would decide which herbs to blow on Jake.

Mrs. Ross was his grandaughter, Indian style. She would give him a proper gift. He would like to have a beef. It would carry him through the winter, and there was still enough sun to dry what he needed, and the rest he would give to his friends.

This evening, when the crow and the coyote had been fed, he sat in his teepee and sang marriage songs. A small fire was burning in the center of the teepee. As lazy smoke drifted up he took out a pipe, put some Indian tobacco in it, and lit it with a coal from the fire. He was at ease with the universe, this was a good omen. he now had time to think about the marriage.

Ku-ken-ish wasn't in any hurry, he knew that Beverly and her mother were aware of all the Indian tribal custom. They wouldn't push him. Still there was something that bothered him, he had an uneasy feeling. He might make a trip to the Cheyenne shaman to see if he had used all of the right signs. It was important that he know all of the sources availabe to him.

That night he had a bad dream, he saw row upon row of covered wagons. There were so many wagons that they covereed the earth like giant grasshoppers. Indians tried desperately to stop them, but on they came. Ku-ken-ish woke up screaming, with his robes wrapped around him. He looked out of his teepee, the cold, blinking stars looked familiar. All of his pets had disappeared, this was a bad omen.

Early in the morning he heard gunshots and saw a flock of crows in the sky. The pet crow must have been among them, because later in the morning it hopped back home. Ku-ken-ish ran and picked it up and carried it into the teepee. He bound its wounds and laid it close to the small fire. Being a true Indian, he was philosophical—a good song, a prayer, and the crow would get well. The old shaman sat a long time that evening. He prayed and sang the old chants. everything had been used to set him right with the world. As if hit by a bolt of lightning, it dawned on him he had forgotten "the people". That was it, of course all Indians considered themselves "the people". Some Indian tribes said that their origin was in the center of the earth. All other people who inhabited the earth were strangers. But not the birds and the animals, or the passing wind. They were part of "the people".

Indians often referred to strangers as vultures. This was his trouble, he had become too muck like the vultures. He had become too interested in owning "things". He would take none of these to his death. Only his ceremonial blankets, drums and rattles would be buried with him, everything else would be left behind. The answer was to have a ceremonial dance, invite his friends, and give all his things away. This would wash away all evil thoughts. Again he consulted the passing wind, it said, "A man must live." True, he would keep only the basic needs of life. Now he felt better, he was at peace, he knew what he had to do. He could now see Beverly, Mrs. Ross, and the man called Jake.

Ku-ken-ish felt that the proper thing to do was to send Jake to the top of Rattlesnake Mountain, spend the night, and bring home a rattlesnake. If he could pass this test he would make a fit husband for her.

Mountain View was about a three hour's drive form the Public Health Hospital. To Jake the trip seemed endless. Mrs. Ross was a careful driver, a little too careful for Jake's style. By the time they pulled off of the main road on to the country road, the shadows of evening were beginning to fall. Clouds of dust rose from Mrs. Ross's car, Jake slowed down so that he could see the road. Suddenly he could see a white house in the distance. This must be the house on the Ross ranch. Beverly had told him about her home, and he was anxious to see what it was like. Mrs. Ross turned up the road that lead to the house. After they had parked, Mrs. Ross got out and actually smiled at Jake. "Well, we are here, you can help Beverly with her things. I have to go to the bunk house. Make yourself at home." Mrs. Ross was making an effort to be friendly, so Jake wondered what she and Beverly had talked about on their trip home. Something certainly had changed the atmosphere.

Beverly was waiting for Jake to help her, she was all smiles.

"Beverly, something has changed. Your mother doesn't seem the same, she was more friendly."

"Yes, mother and I had a good talk on the way home."

"What happened to make her change so?"

"Actually it was a series of things, some good, some not so good. My time in the hospital gave me a chance to think. And several events this summer have had an effect on mother. We found out that some of the things we thought were important fell by the wayside."

"I think I understand." Jake opened the door to help Beverly with her crutches.

"Let me try it without any help, I have to learn sometime." Jake followed behind, then held the door open.

"This is our house, your bedroom will be upstairs, first door to the right. I'm going to use one of the downstairs bedrooms. Let's have something to drink before you get my things. What would you like?"

"I'll take a coke, if you have one."

"We keep most everything." Beverly went to the refrigerator, the going wasn't as easy as she hoped, but she made it. Jake wanted to help, but he knew Beverly was much like her mother in some ways.

"Let's go into the livingroom, I want to prop my leg up for awhile." She plopped down in the largest chair in the room and leaned back. Then Jake brought a footstool over to her, raising her leg gently.

"Thanks, I guess I'm not as strong as I thought. When you finish your coke, why don't you get my bags and your luggage."

When he got back, he wanted to talk, but he could see that the trip had been fatiguing for Beverly.

"I'm going to change and rest for awhile. We usually eat around half past six, but come down any time. There is a TV and a newspaper in the den."

Jake watched Beverly pull herself up. He was also watching for some kind of affection.

"I'm glad you're here, and I'm sure glad to be home. I have a feeling that things are going our way."

"I hope so."

Kissing him gently, Beverly sighed, "I'm tired."

"Let me help you."

"No, I want to do this myself, thanks." A faint smile, and she was gone.

Jake went upstairs, realizing that he, too, was tired. He took off everything but his shorts and lay across the bed. He was asleep in five minutes.

The next thing he knew, someone was knocking on his door. "Jake, Jake," it was Mrs. Ross.

Jake turned over and looked at the ceiling, still half asleep. "Jake!"

"Yes."

"Are you alright?"

"Yes, I'm OK."

"We will be eating in about fifteen minutes."

"Thank you." Jake noticed bath towels at the foot of his bed. Looking out into the hall, he saw that the bathroom door was open. A shower was just what he needed, and to finish off, he turned to cold. This really braced him. He dressed and was downstairs in fifteen minutes. "Hi."

"Hello, Jake. You are a real sleepyhead."

"Yes, I was more tired than I realized. Sleep was what I needed."

Mrs. Ross sat at the head of the table. She put portions of food on a plate and handed it to Jake, then served one for Beverly. Mrs. Ross didn't put much food on her plate. Jake wondered about this family, did they say grace? It was automatic with him, since his father was a minister, but they started eating without it. The food was good, nothing fancy; bacon, eggs, gravy and coffee.

"Jake, after dinner I'll show you the rest of the house, that is, the first floor. Then we can go outside and look around. Also, mother has something to say to you."

"It can wait until we finish our meal," Mr. Ross said.

The interlude was short. "After Beverly shows you around as much as she can, we can go over to see the shaman. I will take you." Jake and Beverly looked at each other, each could tell that the other one was ready. Mrs. Ross stood up, this was the signal that they were excused from the table. Jake stood and walked around to Beverly's chair. As she stood, he pulled the chair gently from under her. He noticed that Mrs. Ross was watching him.

The Ross house had large porches on both the front and the

153

back. The back porch was screened in, and there were some comfortable chairs. This was Mrs. Ross's favorite spot. The house stood on the highest ground of the spread, so from here there was a beautiful view. Looking off in the distance they could see cattle grazing. The heat and the dust created a hazy glow. Nothing was said, they just sat as though enchanted.

The spell broke with a sudden shift in the wind, they all felt it. Mrs. Ross said firmly, "It's time we visited the shaman." Jake turned around to see if Beverly was going, but she didn't move. He realized that this was between him and Mrs. Ross.

The road to the shaman's place was well traveled. In about thirty minutes they came to a barbed wire gate with a sign on it, "Keep Out." Mrs. Ross didn't pay any attention to this. "Jake, would you open the gate?"

"What about the sign?"

"Don't pay any attention to it, Ku-ken-ish knows that we are coming, we will be welcome."

Being familiar with such gates, it was easy for Jake ot open and then close again.

About a mile from the gate they saw a man standing in front of a tent, motioning them forward. Jake felt better. Pulling up to the tent, Mrs. Ross got out and walked over to Ku-ken-ish.

"This young man is the one I was telling you about. he wants to marry Beverly, I want to know if it is right."

Ku-ken-ish parted the tent, "Come in." There were no chairs, but he motioned for them to sit down. "I have consulted with another shaman, also the south wind, my pet crow and coyote. They all tell me to have Jake go to Rattlesnake Mountain, spend the night and bring home a rattlesnake."

Jake wasn't too happy with this, but he didn't say anything.

The old man sang a short song, stood up and shook hands with Mrs. Ross and Jake. "When you are ready, come back. I will show you the way."

Nothing was said on the trip home. As they were getting out of the car, Jake noticed that Mrs. Ross didn't wait to have the door opened. Indian men didn't open doors for their wives. This dual culture made it difficult for some of the young people. Jake usually tried to be flexible in both.

Jake didn't see Beverly around so he sat on the back porch. The world appeared to have quit moving. There was a little breeze rustling the leaves. In the distance a coyote barked. Jake closed his eyes and leaned back in his chair. Then he felt someone touching him.

"Jake, are you asleep?"

"No, I'm just thinking."

Beverly sat close to Jake, and reached over and took his hand. "How did it go between you and Ku-ken-ish?"

"It didn't last long. He said I have to spend the night on Rattlesnake Mountain. Are there really rattlesnakes up ther?"

"Yes, I've heard men talk about it, they say it isn't so bad. You should wear boots, and take a forked stick to pin down the snake. It's important that you start before it gets dark. Rattlesnakes have to be disturbed before they will strike. if you follow Ku-ken-ish you will be safe, because he knows the path very well. Also, take stick matches, a hunting knife, and something to eat. It will be a long night."

"I don't have a knife."

"I'll get you one. And I have a back pack with a sleeping bag that you can use."

"Thanks. What else do I need to know?"

"After you set up your camp, gather some wood. Be careful, because rattlers often lie under sticks or anything they can get under. Always use your forked stick to turn over anything before you pick it up. Build a fire at three points around your camp. Light them as it gets dark and let them burn all night. This will keep the rattlers away. They seldom look for trouble, but don't take any chances.

"I'm sure Ku-ken-ish will take you up the mountain. He will also come up in the morning after the sun comes up, follow him again when he comes down. The best time for you to get a snake will be as soon as the sun comes up, and the heat sets in. Rattlers always sun for awhile before crawling under something cool."

"Anything else?"

"No, I don't think so."

"Thanks for the help, I think I can do the job."

"I know you can, just don't take any chances. Oh yes, there is one more thing. Take along a burlap sack to put the rattler in after you pin it down with your forked stick. You can hold him behind the head, so he can't turn on you. Take a leather thong to wrap around the top of the sack, and you can tie it to the stick. Most snake hunters don't worry much after they have the snake in the bag, however, since this is your first hunt, you needn't feel bad about using the stick to keep the bag away from your body."

"Sounds easy enough. I hope I don't get buck fever."

"I think you will make it alright, just keep your cool."

"What time does your mother go to bed?"

Beverly held her wristwatch up to the light from the house, "It's about ten o'clock. Mother usually listenes to the news, and reads awhile in bed before going to sleep."

No sooner had Beverly finished than her mother called, "Beverly."

"Out here, Mother."

Mrs. Ross came over to Beverly and kissed her cheek. "Good night, Jake. Do you have everything you need?"

"Yes. Thank you. I've been thinking about the night on Rattlesnake Mountain.

"Yes, I'm sure you have. Well, good night." That was all, she didn't linger.

After awhile Beverly asked, "Jake, where do you want to live after we are married?"

Jake rememberd what his father had told him. He was pleased that Beverly was taking their plans for granted. "Why don't we go out under the stars. You could stretch out, and we could talk, just talk."

"Alright. There's a blanket in a chair in the livingroom, we could spread it out on the grass."

Jake didn't wait, he was up and had the blanket. Feeling like superman, he reached down and picked Beverly up up in his arms. He carried her toward a large tree, "Prop yourself up by this tree while I spread the blanket."

They lay on their backs looking into the sky. The stars were fairly dancing.

"I've been thinking about going to the University of Oklahoma so you would be closer home."

"But what about you? You would be further from your home in Kansas."

"Really, it isn't so far from Oklahoma City, it's about three and a half hours."

"I know where we can get an apartment in Norman. We could move in after our honeymoon trip. Mother said she wanted to give

156

us a trip as a gift."

Jake remembered what his father told him would happen, Beverly and her mother had been making plans. So far, they were alright with him. He askd Beverly, "Where do you want to go on our honeymoon?"

"I've always wanted to make a trip to San Francisco."

"That should be nice. If we fly it will take us three hours, if we drive it will take three days."

They were silent agian.

Beverly looked at Jake, "When are you going to the mountain?"

"I thought I would go over to the shaman's tomorrow, the sooner the better. I'll go after breakfast, he migh be in a good mood." Jake propped himself up on his elbows close to Beverly. "I love you so much, I'm ready for our marriage."

"I also am ready." Beverly reached up to Jake's face and pulled it down to hers. They were locked in a deep embrace. Then they fell apart and rolled on their backs. The sky fairly sparkled, it was as though they could reach up into the milky way and grab a handfull of stars. Beverly reached for Jake's hand and kissed it. Jake responded by doing the same thing to Beverly's hand.

"I think we should go in. We are in love, but not yet lovers. When I become your bride, I want you to be the first man that has made love to me." Jake was aware that his face was burning. He was tongue-tied.

"Have I said something wrong, Jake?"

"No, I still have a lot to learn. I don't know if I will make a good husband or not."

"We can both learn together."

Jake stood up and carried Beverly to her bedroom. He placed her in a chaise lounge. Jake hadn't been in her room before. It was like a fairyland; lacy curtains, a four-poster bed, a soft carpet, all in white. This was too much for a country boy. Kissing her gently, he left. His thoughts were racing. "Bring on the rattlesnake," he mumbled to himself.

Jake was tired, and soon fell asleep. His dream was as real as life. He was back with the shaman talking about cures for rattlesnake bites. Mrs. Ross walked into the tent holding a rattler and singing. Jake flinched, and the old man grinned. "The snake won't hurt her because she is a witch, and it won't hurt you because

157

she has witched the snake."

Jake awoke with the feeling that he had been moaning, and he wondered if anyone heard him. He listened, but there wasn't a sound in the house, only the wind in the eaves.

The next sound was of someone calling, "Jake, Jake." This was the same as yesterday.

"Yes."

"It's breakfast time."

"I'll be down in a few minutes." While he was dressing he thought about the shaman, he was anxious to get started. Beverly and her mother were waiting at the bottom of the stairs.

"I'm ready for breakfast, and I'm ready to see the shaman." Beverly and her mother looked at each other and grinned. Jake helped Beverly into her chair. Mrs. Ross brought in pancakes and eggs. She loved to cook, and with a man in the house, she had an extra reason.

Jake said, "I would like to drive over after breakfast and talk to the shaman."

"You can use the blue pickup," Mrs. Ross said. "It's parked over by the horse stables just west of here. You can't miss it, it's painted blue. The rest of the outbuildings are painted red and white. The painter had had too much to drink, he and his helpers painted it blue before I could stop them. He said he would give me a discount because of the mistake."

"Did he?"

"Yes, but it didn't amount to much. You will find the keys to the pickup in the bunkhouse, they are marked according to the color of the pickup."

"Everything in order!"

"Yes, that's the way I am."

"Would you excuse me, I'm anxious to get started."

The instructions had been very exact. Jake found the keys and the pickup, and was on his way.

The old shaman wasn't as anxious as Jake. He had been up most of the night with a man who had been witched by his mother-in-law. Jake argued, "If we make plans today, I thought I could go up the mountain tomorrow. After we make our plans let's go to town, I want to buy you some food supplies."

This was like music to Ku-ken-ish, he was ready for a talk. "Sit down, I will get you some coffee."

158

"Thanks."

They sat on the floor facing each other. Jake took a sip of the coffee, it was strong and hot, but he didn't flinch. "It's good."

"Yes, it's good. I buy Folgers, it's the best. Indians like their coffee strong and black."

"That they do."

"I have consulted the stars, I think tomorrow would be a good day to go to the mountain."

"I'm ready. Beverly has mentioned some of the things that I should take."

The old man grumbled, "Women don't know anything about a man's job."

Jake smiled. But the shaman didn't make a big deal of the remarks from Beverly, he didn't want to antagonize the Ross family.

"What time can you come over tomorrow morning?"

"The Ross family eats early, so I can be over here whenever you want to start."

"Come over when the rooster crows three times."

"What time is that?"

"The only time I know is when the sun comes up and the rooster crows."

"I will be ready."

"Go in peace."

Jake knew that this was a dismissal. The old shaman was sitting, legs crossed, eyes closed. Jake walked out, climbed into the blue pickup and headed for Beverly's.

As Jake pulled into the yard he noticed Beverly standing on the porch. Suddenly he felt a chill in his body. He was alright, so it must be some omen. He didn't like it. He hadn't thought much about all of the signs that the shaman felt were so important. He felt depressed. But walking toward Beverly he began to feel better. She put another dimension in his life, this is what it was all about.

"How did it go?"

"Alright. I need to know something about Indian time. What time is it when the rooster crows three times?"

Beverly smiled. Turning her head she stifled a laugh.

"What's funny?"

"I'm sorry, it just seems funny that you don't know. When the

159

rooster crows three times, means whenever you get where you are going. It is no special time."

"I see, thanks. Oh, I forgot something.

"What?"

I told the shaman I would take him to town to buy him some supplies. When I left I was thinking about something else, and he seemed to be in deep meditation."

"Don't worry, the shaman seldom leaves his camp, and when he does it is usually in the late afternoon. Come on, let's have lunch, you have had a busy morning. We will talk about the shaman after we eat."

"I'm ready."

Mrs. Ross wasn't home, she had gone to another rancher's to buy some heifers. The house was cool, there was a nice breeze coming in the kitchen door. Mrs. Ross had built a breakfast nook in the corner. She had put in a picture window so that she could look out and enjoy the view. The ranch was her pride and joy, next to Beverly.

Beverly had bathed and put on her favorite scent. She wore white slacks and blouse, with a red sash. The effect was perfect. Jake sat down in the breakfast nook almost breathless.

"What's the matter?"

"You are so beautiful."

"The beauty is all for you."

Jake reached over and took her hand. Beverly moved over to his side. They slid into each other's arms as naturally as breathing. "Wow! One more kiss and then we eat." Jake felt he was on cloud nine.

Beverly had fixed ham and cheese sandwiches with chips. She had put a large pitcher of milk in front of Jake and a salad that she knew he liked.

"Is this the way it will be when we get married?"

"I hope so, but don't forget we will have to start off in a small way."

"Just as long as we have each other, it will be perfect."

Jake was a hearty and fast eater. He watched while Beverly finished her lunch. "What are you thinking?"

"I'm thinking I'll clean up the table while you go out and sit on the porch. I'll join you in a few minutes."

"On one condition."

160

"What's that?"

"You give me a hug and a kiss."

"That sounds good to me."

Jake strolled out on the long porch and sat down in the swing. It seemed to him that he was always waiting. He wondered if he would ever become Beverly's husband.

When Beverly came out Jake said, "Let's take a blanket and lie under the big oak tree. We can talk and plan."

"Don't forget the shaman."

"I won't." Jake thought to himself how much Beverly was like her mother, and wondered if they would have problems with the decisions that would come up in their lives.

Beverly said, "I'll go in and get a blanket."

Jake stood up when she came out. He reached for the blanket and held the screen door open. She was managing her crutches easily, you could see the remains of a tree house.

Beverly was remembering a swing in this very tree. As a child he had climbed this tree many times, and if you looked closely, you could see the remains of a tree house.

"What are you thinking, Beverly?"

"About all of the things that happened to me when I was growing up."

"What do you mean?"

Beverly began telling Jake about all the hours she had spent in this very spot as a child, and what it meant to her. "I will have mixed feelings about leaving home.'

"But Beverly, you can always come back. Our marriage will not cut you off from your home. I want you to come home as often as possible. I know how much it means to you." Beverly wasn't a sentimental girl, but home was a special place. She knew she was fortunate to have had such a happy childhood.

"Mother says that when a girl marries, she shouldn't hold on to the past, she should leave her mother and father and give herself to her husband."

They were both quiet.

"Say, let's go get the shaman." Beverly grabbed the blanket and headed for the blue pickup. She was so excited that she momentarily forgot her cast.

"Hey, don't forget your crutches."

This cracked them up.

161

"You are getting along real well. how much longer do you have to wear the cast?"

"Two weeks."

When they arrived at the shaman's camp, polite exchanges were made, then Jake asked, "Are you ready to get your supplies?"

"I'm ready." Ku-ken-ish looked pleased. He didn't like to go by himself. White people made him uneasy, and they always asked stupid questins. With Jake and Beverly he felt at ease.

The store was almost empty at this time of th day. He gave the list to the owner, then wandered over to the cold drink box. He got himself a red one, strawberry was a favorit with all Indians.

On the way back the old shaman sang to himself, he was at peace. Jake helped unload the truck, then the shaman said, "Come over tomorrow, we will go to the mountain." Again, just like yesterday, Jake felt a chill. It was unreal.

The evening was uneventful. Jake packed the few things he would take along on his trip. He went to bed early, he wanted to be on top of everything. But he didn't sleep well, he kept dreaming about snakes. When one big rattler came after him, he jerked and rolled out of bed. He wondered if anyone heard him fall. he listened, but he could hear only the familiar night sounds, and the gentle sound of the wind in the eaves. He crawled back into bed.

Someone was knocking on his door.

"Yes?"

"It's time for breakfast."

"Thanks."

This was the day he climbed the mountain. He didn't have any misgivings about it, but the dream had shaken him.

Beverly and her mother had started eating. "We didn't wait. Mother has to leave in a few minutes, and she wanted me to eat with her."

"That's alright." Just the same, he could feel the hair on the back of his neck bristle.

"Are you all ready? You don't seem too anxious."

"No, I had a bad dream last night, I guess it upset me."

"What was it about?"

"Snakes."

162

"You can ask the shaman about your dream."

"Yes, I will."

They finished in silence. Only the clicking of their cups into their saucers was noticeable.

"Fred is going to drive us over this morning, I would, but the cast gets in my way."

"I know." Jake was obviously glum.

"I'm going with you and Fred. I wish I could go with you to the mountain." Beverly really meant what she said, but somehow the words had a hollow ring.

"I wish you could too, but, as you know, this is supposed to be my test."

"Let's go, mother will clean up when she gets back.

Beverly hobbled along on her crutches. Jake had his backpack in place and was carrying his supplies. In the morning's haze they looked like two lost souls marching off into the unknown.

Fred was waiting at the blue pickup. Jake threw his supplies in the back, and helped Beverly into the truck. Fred was full of good humor, this didn't give Jake and Beverly a chance to talk. But Fred's incessant chatter did lift some of the tension.

When they arrived at the shaman's, Jake flipped open the car door and helped Beverly climb out. Fred helped Jake with his things. "You have enough food and supplies to last a long time, how long are you going to stay?"

"One night."

"Just one night?"

"That's all."

Fred went over to the shaman, shook his hand and returned to the truck mumbling something to himself.

Jake and Beverly walked over to the shaman, greeting him Indian style with the dead-fish handshake.

"Come in." The old man turned around and went into the tent. Beverly had a hard time getting down to the ground. Jake didn't know if he was supposed to help her or not, the shaman might think less of him.

Jake turned to Ku-ken-ish, "Something has changed. I had a dream last night, a bad one."

"About snakes?"

"Yes, how did you know?"

"I had a strange dream also."

163

"About what?"

"White medicine men and car salesmen."

Jake smiled, "That must have been some dream. I don't guess you have any use for either."

"No. White medicine men always tell you what they don't know, they want you to go to another one. They don't treat everything. They have specialists in everything. Me, I treat everything."

"What about the car salesmen?"

"One came out to my place one time and tried to sell me a car, said he would trade me a car for my land."

"What did you do?"

"I took my deer rifle out and shot over his head. The last I saw of him, he was running down the road."

The stories were enough to break the spell, they were all more relaxed. It looked as though it was going to be a good day.

"I am ready," the shaman said. He didn't have much gear. He was only going as a guide, and would return after he had shown Jake where to make camp.

In the background Jake could see Fred waiting by the pickup. He had the hood up and was looking at the motor. He wasn't fooling anyone, they knew it was just a way to avoid the tension.

Jake turned to Beverly, pulling her into his arms. Suddenly he felt a chill. "Damn it."

Beverly pulled away, "What's the matter?"

"It's nothing between us. But this is the third time I've had this feeling, it's like a cold chill." Again Beverly reminded him to ask the shaman.

Jake felt himself becoming irritated. "Let's go!" They headed toward the mountain. Looking back, Jake could see the dust from the pickup. Now the world around them seemed fresh and unspoiled by so-called civilization.

Ku-ken-ish was one of the last of his family, and had inherited all of their property. It had stayed the same, a large tract of land as originally created.

They walked along, not saying anything. Finally the old man said, "Observe the landmarks so that you can find your way out. And from now on, be careful where you step, we are nearing rattlesnake country. They won't hurt you unless you step on them, or frighten them while they are asleep."

Then they heard that terrible rattling sound that only a rattlere can make. Jake saw the rattler's tail standing upright, and heard other rattlers making their hollow sound. The old shaman wasn't quick enough, the rattler had struck. He went down holding his leg. Jake picked up a club and beat the snake to a pulp.

"Come quick. Take a knife and cut my pant's leg. Then cut my leg with your knife, and suck out the poison. It's the only way."

Jake did as he was told. He put a tourniquet above the bite, cut the leg and let it bleed. He couldn't bring himself to suck out the poison.

"Hurry, or it will be too late!"

Finally Jake bent over and placed his mouth over the bite. It made him sick.

"It won't hurt you, spit it out."

Again Jake did as he was told.

"It is too late," said Ku-ken-ish.

Jake didn't give up, he kept the blood flowing by sucking. He could feel the old man relax. Turning, he could see that the old man's face was ashen, life was going out of his body. Jake kept working, then the chill returned. This time he knew the shaman was dead. In shock, he sat down on a rock, and finally he began to cry. He realized something had to be done, so he stretched out the old man, took the blanket from his pack and rolled the shaman in it. He tied both ends with a rope to keep out the birds and animals. He left everything and started back on a dead run.

After it was all over he realized he probably couldn't do it again. Beverly told him later that he had run all the way back to her house.

He had told Fred, "The shaman is dead, a snake got him." A search party from the ranch had found Ku-ken-ish along the trail. They were philosophical, the only comment they made was, "His time had come."

Jake felt their dream of the future had ended. Beverly didn't need to tell him, he saw it in her eyes. Finally, Mrs. Ross came to his room. Her words were slow in coming. "We like you, we think you would make a good husband for Beverly. But these people think you brought them bad luck. I don't, it was just an accident. I think it best that you return home to your people. Come back sometime later." Instead of great happiness that a wedding brings, only sorrow. Jake said, "I want to be alone. I'll be starting home as soon as I pack."

"I understand."Mrs. Ross closed the door softly. Jake heard the familiar sound of the wind in the eaves. He would remember this sound for the rest of his life.

Jake packed, leaving the gifts that he had brought. Looking sadly out the window, he could see people gathering.

Beverly was waiting at the foot of the stairs, and went on her crutches with him to the car. Jake threw all of his belongings in the back seat. Facing each other they could only see the love they felt. They hung on each other in a life-giving embrace. Jake knew he had to get going, he couldn't stand anymore. Getting into his volkswagon he looked at Beverly, tears were running down her cheeks. She leaned over and gave him a tender kiss.

Starting the car, Jake heard Beverly say, "I'll see you next summer." As he drove off down the dusty road they both knew next summer would never come.

9

Driving had always given Jake a time for reflection, a time to think things through. So much had happened, the ramifications on his life would be evident.

His mind drifted to his father; he was loving, giving, really a very special person, a truly remarkable man. "How could my dad believe, and live with, such contradictions; love your enemies, the poor shall inherit the earth. I just don't understand...the preaching and reality just don't mesh."

Jake had not studied all of the religions of the world, but he knew that the protestant religion was one of the smaller ones. For Jake, religion should be a doing, compassionate part of an individual. There was no need to meet with others, talking about the grace of God. People could judge you by your good works. This made sense to Jake.

Fortunately, Jake's mind had been computerized, driving was mechanical. The events of the summer were strong in his memory; school, Darla, Mary Marie, Joy, Beverly, the death of the shaman. It was like a dream, yet he knew it was real. First he recalled the most recent events, the death of the shaman, then to Beverly, he could almost reach out and touch her, her warmth, her style so different and yet so natural.

Joy was such a contrast, she had sand, a woman to walk down the road of life with. Her beauty was in her control, he recalled her majestic walk.

Mary Marie, ah, there was a real female. Everything about

167

her was beautiful, a perfect model for Miss America. She had some psychological scars, but, for the most part, she handled them well. Money was a part of her, a true heiress, she had it all. Her husband would have to be a very special person to handle it.

Then there was Darla, she just didn't interest him anymore. It had been both exciting and frightening to be persued by her.

Jake was overwhelmed by the females in his life, in this he included his mother. He realized he would welcome some of the shaman's wisdom. He had lived life with zest and pleasure, now there would be a short interval of reckoning.

The miles rolled by. It was a hot day, off to the west, dark clouds were forming. When the cool breezes from the north hit the warm, moist air from the south it meant trouble, whether in the form of a hail storm or a tornado. Hail storms were not killers, but they would strip trees of their leaves, dent automobiles, knock over wheat. Hail storms did a lot of damage.

Tornados were something else. They killed people and animals, and destroyed property. Tornados were respected by most farmers, they had cellars or 'fraid holes'. The townspeople were a little more indifferent, but they often paid for this show of bravery.

Jake's mind was wandering, "Strange, while I was in school all I could think about was getting out. I'm a little older now, and I feel heavy, as if old man time was sitting on my left shoulder."

Jake blinked his eyes and shook his head, he was getting sleepy. His body wanted to relax, but he needed his mind to work for him. He was eager to get home and talk to his mother and dad.

The storm was getting closer, it seemed to be trying to head him off. Still, he was not too far from home. Suddenly his car leaped forward. That was strange, he glanced in his rear view mirror to see if the Highway Patrol was following him. Nothing, absolutely nothing.

Now it was really getting dark, he felt like he was in a giant void. Now he was frightened, what was going on? It was a race, would he beat the storm to his house, or would it beat him? These tornados in Oklahoma and Kansas would put the fear of God in you.

It was little wonder that the storm had hit and moved east by the time Jake arrived home. When he drove into the yard, only the fence was left. Stunned, he walked over to where the house had stood, there was nothing, total destruction. Only stumps of branches were left of the trees. One tree had been pulled from the ground, there was a gaping hole. He opened the door to the cellar, only a damp smell came out, it was empty. Jake was satisfied that his parents had taken shelter elsewhere.

Dumbfounded, dazed, Jake stumbled to his car. His power of reasoning had left him. Resting his head on the steering wheel, breathing deeply, he felt like the oxygen had been sucked out of him. After a short period of time his breathing returned to normal, slowly his mind cleared.

Jake knew what he had to do. His parents were probably with others who had found themselves in the same situation. He felt that if he could find Joy, she would know something.

Jake drove to the Hollman's. There was nothing standing. He walked slowly to where the house had stood, there was only the foundation, with parts of the plumbing pointing towards the sky.

"My God, where is everyone?" He shook his head in disbelief, there must be something.

Suddenly he was startled by a thumping noise from what looked like a giant ball of lumber. There were also pieces of farm equipment and parts of the tin barn, it was like something out of a science fiction story.

Walking toward the noise it became louder, and he heard a voice calling, "Help! Hello? Help...help."

Jake's adrenalin started flowing, he was like a wild man, the boards flew as he tossed them aside. He was stopped by some large beams crisscrosing the rest of the pile. Now he was close enough to call out, "Are you under the beams of wood?"

"Yes, we are in the cellar."

"Who?"

"Me."

"Who is me?"

"Joy."

"Who else?"

"Your father and mother."

"Good. Are you hurt or anything?"

"No, we are alright, all we need is to get out of this cellar. If the beams are too heavy, there is a tractor in the barn with a winch. Is the barn still there?"

"Yes, I'll get the tractor, you stay where you are." He realized what a dumb statement that was. The barn was intact, it was built like a fortress against a bluff. It was all cement and rock, only a direct hit from a field piece could have destroyed it.

Jake found the tractor and drove it to the cellar. Releasing the coil of wire from the winch, he wrapped it around the largest beam, set the brakes on the tractor and turned on the winch. With a roar the tractor's great torque pulled off the beam as if it were a toy. He did the same thing to all of the larger pieces. When he pulled the last piece off of the cellar, the door popped open, and Joy and his parents climbed out. They were gasping for fresh air, their lungs were almost out of oxygen.

They all ran toward Jake. Joy threw her arms around him, and they hung on to each other as if they were afraid they would lose each other. Releasing Joy he did the same thing with his mother and father, each person was solid gold. Finally satisfied, Jake turned toward Joy, "Where are the others?"

"The Hollmans went to town before the storm, I'm sure they took shelter someplace in town."

"After I put the tractor in the barn, I want to hear all about the storm and you."

Before Jake could move again there were flashes of lightning and a loud crash of thunder. The clouds were gathering with streaks of rainbow colors. It was so startling that they stopped in their tracks...four people looking toward the heavens, awe written on their faces. A group of clouds formed the head of the shaman.

"Oh no, it couldn't be."

"What's the matter, Jake?"

"It's the shaman."

"What do you mean?"

"Not now, later. There is too much to tell."

Jake couldn't move, his eyes were transfixed on the sky. Clearly there was a voice saying, "Beverly is not for you, find one of your kind."

"Did you hear that?"

"Hear what?"

"The voice from the clouds."

"We didn't hear anything."

As suddenly as the storm clouds had appeared they split and moved on. Still Jake didn't move. His questions had been partially answered.

"What is it, Jake?" his father asked.

"It's a long story. When we find a place to stay I will tell you. Our next job is to find the Hollmans." The only transportation was Jake's volkswagon, so they all piled in.

They spent the rest of the day helping people gather up their belongings. Toward evening they saw the Hollmans in the distance, there was more yelling, more hugging and crying. Happiness was the theme, they had survived.

That evening they bedded down in the National Guard Armory, there were cots set up for all who needed them. A Red Cross first aid station fed them and gave them toilet articles. They also gave them food and steaming cups of coffee

The townspeople were in a state of shock. Those who had not lost anything did everything to lend a hand where it was needed.

After their meal, Jake managed to get his mother and father into a corner of the large room. He explained to them about his trip, the death of the shaman and the voice from the clouds. He had just left his parents when the loudspeaker announced a long distance call for Jake Hawkins. He hurried to the information desk.

"I'm Jake Hawkins."

The volunteer Red Cross worker pointed to the battery of telephones, "Take your call on number five." Jake wondered what else could happen. He lifted the telephone off of the cradle, "Hello?"

"Hello, is that you, Jake?"

"Yes, Mary Marie," he recognized her voice.

"You guessed it. I heard all about the storm, are you alright?"

"Yes, we are safe."

"What about the storm?"

"It blew our house away. We are in a National Guard Armory, we'll have to find a place to live."

There was a long pause, "Jake, I'm leaving tomorrow for Pittsburgh. I had a call from my uncle and he said there were some financial matters that need my authorization. He also wants to go to Europe and settle some of my international investments."

"Will you be gone for a long time?"

"I really don't know, Uncle Charles didn't say."

"What about us?"

Again there was a long pause. "Jake, I know I care about

171

you as much as I could any man. I have thought a lot about us. I think our meeting was a very beautiful, summer interlude, that's all." Then Mary Marie put Jake on the spot, "Do you want to marry me?"

"I love you very much but I have four years of college, perhaps after that."

"OK, Jake." The voice sounded distant, "I love you, too. Why don't we just walk away from it? Maybe, just maybe, we can get together after you finish college."

"Yes, that's the answer. Take care on your trip, and send me a postcard. I love you, I always will."

"Me too."

With the click of the phone, they both knew it was over, they had made empty promises.

His father was the first to notice, "Something wrong, Jake?"

"It was Mary Marie, she's off on a trip to Europe."

"It was nice of her to call. I felt that you really liked Mary Marie."

"I did, I guess the time wasn't right."

Before they had bedded down for the night, Jacob's congregation swarmed around and announced, "We will start building you a new house tomorrow, we have everyone lined up. Can you help, Jake?"

"Yes, I can, but my dad isn't supposed to do any heavy work."

"Does your family have a place to stay?"

"Yes, mother has talked to her parents, and they want us to stay with them."

Jake managed to get Joy off from the others. "What about you? Where will you stay?"

"The Hollman's have already found a temporary house for us."

"That's great." Jake could feel his heart beating faster, he took a deep breath. "Joy, There is something else."

"Yes?"

"Will you marry me?"

"You mean it?"

"With all my heart. Of course, I still have my college education before me."

"I'll work."

"Yes, we'll both work."

172

They were engulfed in each others arms. Suddenly there was a flash of lightning and a clap of thunder. They ran to the door, there was a flash of lightning as bright as day. A voice said, "She is the one."

There was a smile on Jake's face, "Did you hear the voice?"

"No. Are you alright?"

"I never felt better. Come on, let's tell everyone." Jake requested the mike. "Everyone, I have a very important announcement, Joy and I are going to get married!"

Everyone was clapping and smiling. Jake and Joy were busy receiving congratulations and best wishes.

The shaman had the last word. There was a loud clap of thunder that sounded like laughter. Jake was the only one who understood. It would be his secret.